S0-CNG-441

SWEET SURRENDER

•

Janet Cookson

PUBLIC LIBRARY OF ENID
and GARFIELD COUNTY
PO BOX 8002
ENID, OK 73702

AVALON BOOKS
NEW YORK

© Copyright 1999 by Janet Cookson
Library of Congress Catalog Card Number: 99-90979
ISBN 0-8034-9384-3
All rights reserved.
All the characters in this book are fictitious,
and any resemblance to actual persons,
living or dead, is purely coincidental.
Published by Thomas Bouregy & Co., Inc.
401 Lafayette Street, New York, NY 10003

PRINTED IN THE UNITED STATES OF AMERICA
ON ACID-FREE PAPER
BY HADDON CRAFTSMEN, BLOOMSBURG, PENNSYLVANIA

SWEET SURRENDER

Chapter One

Kathryn Beaumont shivered in the cool, night air and wondered whether to break into Hollinswood Manor or to go home and forget the whole thing. The open window, a dark void, beckoned invitingly. It would be so easy to slip into the rear porch and gain access to the rest of the empty property. She could check out each room in turn, then leave, no one the wiser. Surely she had a right to see what the workmen were doing to this beautiful old house? Why, not so long ago she'd had the run of the place.

A gust of wind cut through her, causing her to pull her woollen hat firmly into place over her wiry, coppery curls. No use standing around freezing to death, she decided. It's now or never.

Kathryn thrust her arms through the gap, head following. The sill dug into her flat stomach as she lifted her feet off the ground and pushed herself forward. Tipping over she reached forward confidently, searching for something to break her fall.

What she found was a pair of large male hands.

She screamed as fingers threaded tightly through hers and pulled her forward. She fell, her face sliding against the hard wall of a chest clothed in silken material. Then the rest of her body followed, her knees impacting with well muscled thighs.

Her unknown assailant gave a muffled groan, releasing her hands. She recoiled as though touching fire and lost her balance. Falling sideways, she cried out as her elbows and knees crunched against the quarry tiled floor.

Immediately she moved onto her knees, only to fall back on her heels in shock as the porch was flooded with light.

A man in maroon silk pajamas was sitting on the edge of an old armchair peering down at her.

Auburn, spiky hair, worn longish, framed a face bleached by the pale light from the lamp beside him. Dark eyebrows were raised over slanting gray eyes silvered by the light and outlined by thick, black lashes. It was a finely sculptured face. The skin was stretched tautly across high cheekbones while the nose was aquiline and etched by strong lines which led to lips set in a very straight line.

What extraordinary bone structure, she thought momentarily. It gave his face a predatory, almost wolfish appearance. She shivered, her eyes locked into his, held by the intensity of his gaze like a wild creature transfixed by a beam of light.

His hand moved forward without warning and she flinched. A second later he had torn her woollen hat from her head, and her hair, loosened from its knot, tumbled down in a cloud of russet curls. She gasped, the spell broken. He dangled the hat in front of him then tossed it contemptuously to one side.

"Do you mind," she snapped, stung into words, "that's my hat."

"Do you mind," he countered, "this is my house."

"Your house?" To her annoyance her voice came out as a plaintive squeak. What on earth had she done? She'd blundered across the new owner himself. She'd embarrass the family, jeopardize their position . . . .

"I think you'd better get up!" She rose swiftly, uncomfortably aware of his scrutiny as his eyes swept over her and came to rest on her face, taking in the brown eyes and dark brows that contrasted so sharply with the creaminess of her skin.

"I hope you've seen enough," Kathryn said tartly. She might be in an awkward position, but that was no reason to let the man look her over as though she were in a livestock show.

She was aware of a sudden lightening of the atmosphere as his lips curved into a smile. "I think so. I must say, you don't look like a professional burglar."

"I'm nothing of the kind." She bit back a further retort, reminding herself of the delicate position she was in. Defending herself was one thing, but she couldn't afford to antagonize the man who had just bought the Manor estate and now controlled the land on which the family business depended. She must make sure he did not take the matter further. Above all he must not discover her connection to Hollinswood Stables.

Perhaps a conciliatory approach? Chewing her lower lip, she attempted to school her features into a friendly smile. He seemed singularly unimpressed, his glance dismissive as he rose and looked down at her. As a tall woman she was surprised at how much he towered over her, and she steeled herself to meet his gaze.

"Come into the kitchen, please. I think you owe me an explanation." He turned and led the way out of the porch.

Don't wait for my agreement, Kathryn thought resentfully. Do order me about like your bond servant. She glanced uncertainly at the still open window. A sudden image of herself leaping through it and running down the driveway entered her mind. It looked easy enough in the movies.

"Don't even think it."

Kathryn started at his harsh tone and saw him observing her from the doorway with narrow-eyed scrutiny. She followed him through into the kitchen.

He flicked on the light, revealing a room in which every available surface was piled high with cartons and packing cases. To her relief Kathryn noticed that the huge Yorkshire range set deep into the chimney breast was still in use, its surfaces gleaming from years of assiduous blackleading, heat emanating from its glowing coals. Instinctively she moved toward it, hands outstretched, as though turning to an old friend for comfort.

"Sit down."

"Please," Kathryn added under her breath as she sank into the armchair next to the range, its broken springs groaning as she leaned forward, knees together and backbone rigid, uncomfortably aware that she must look like some recalcitrant pupil in the principal's study.

"What would you like to drink—Scotch or Scotch?"

His voice was low-timbred, and for the first time she realized there was a lilt to it, an inflection that she could not define for the moment.

She opened her lips to refuse, then became aware of the slight tremor in her hands and the cold that streamed through her bones. She was, she supposed, suffering from shock.

"Scotch will be fine," she assented, low-voiced. She watched surreptitiously as he crossed the room, his movements remarkably fluid for such a tall man as he negotiated a path through the carton-strewn floor to reach a table laden with a bottle of Scotch and squat cut-glass tumblers.

Maroon silk pajamas, indeed! He'll have to get used to warmer clothing if he's to face a winter in the North of England, Kathryn thought sourly. She averted her eyes as he brought her drink over, though she noticed the slenderness of the long fingers that curled around the glass, the well-shaped hand, and the dusting of fine, dark hairs on the wrist.

"Thanks." She took the offered glass and drank eagerly and deeply, forgetting that it was neat whiskey. As the liquid fired through her blood, she coughed and spluttered, slipping off her jacket as her body was suffused with unexpected warmth.

Inwardly she winced at her gauche behavior, conscious of his scrutiny as a red flush crested the neckline of her T-shirt. Why, oh why, did she have to have such transparent skin? And why was this man hovering so close, dissecting her with those extraordinary silver eyes as though she were some laboratory specimen?

She looked up with a dark glance of her own as amusement, swiftly controlled, fleeted across his angular features. "Well," he said solemnly, "whatever else you are, you're certainly no boozer, Miss . . . ?"

Thank goodness her surname was different from the rest of the family! She could introduce herself with impunity. "My name is Kathryn Beaumont."

Her hands twisted in her lap as she looked pointedly away from his questioning gaze. To her relief he turned aside, words brisk, as he strode toward the small moquette armchair opposite.

"Well, Miss Beaumont, perhaps you'd like to explain yourself."

"When I've found out who you are!"

"I'm Gerard Fitzalan."

Kathryn drew suddenly dampened palms down her thighs, the innocuous words confirming what she had feared since he had professed ownership of the Manor. "So . . . you own Fitzalan Enterprises?" she inquired, dry-mouthed.

"I do. And you're trying to avoid my question."

Her jaw set. "I have nothing to hide." At least not much, she amended silently as she attempted to put her thoughts in order. She drew a steadying breath. "It—it's all quite innocent, really. I'd heard that the Manor had been sold to your company, and I was curious about the renovations. On impulse I just . . . well, slipped inside to have a look." Goodness, it sounded lame, though it was, at its most basic, the truth.

"Mmm." His tone was skeptical. "Why didn't you ask my foreman to show you around during the day?"

"Well, I've been in France all summer. I only returned today. When I heard about the sale I wandered up to have a look at the old place."

"And just happened to find a conveniently open window?"

"I've been shinning in and out of that window for years!" She had sparked back a reply before realizing the folly of her words. Stupid, stupid! her mind shrieked. Her nerves might be jangled, but it was no excuse for losing control of her brain!

"So . . ." He shifted position, his eyes scanning her face. "You started on a life of crime at an early age. Been profitable has it?"

"Don't be ridiculous! I, well, I . . ." It was no use, she'd have to disclose a little more than she'd intended. The sooner she satisfied this man's curiosity, the sooner she could leave. She attempted a placatory smile. "You see, Lady Alice Cardew, the previous owner of the Manor, needed a good deal of help in her old age, so the village set up a support system. She could never hear the doorbell—too deaf—so it was quicker to enter through the porch window. It's been jammed open for years, by the way . . ." She stumbled to a halt, suddenly conscious that she was rambling.

He homed in on her disquiet with, "I'm gratified to know you're kind to little old ladies. How are you with puppies?"

"Fine," she rapped. "How are you with manners?" She turned away from his dark frown, pleased at having scored one small point against him and quite unprepared for his next broadside.

"You must live close by to be part of such community highjinks. How close exactly?"

No way could she reveal her address! "Not too close, no—the, er—next valley, actually." She stared into the range, her cheeks the color of the banked-up fire as she wished, just for once, that she could lie convincingly.

"I see." The words were loaded, but to her surprise he did not follow up his advantage, instead changing tack with, "Did you expect to find the house unoccupied?"

"Obviously," she confirmed. Did he think she'd intended to blunder into him? Engineered the whole charade in order to make contact with the handsome new owner of the Manor?

"Of course, the house would have been empty," he went on musingly, "if I hadn't flown in unexpectedly from New York."

Pity. The unspoken word hung in the air between them, and Kathryn had an uncanny feeling that Gerard Fitzalan knew all too well what she was thinking. With one languid movement he reached for his glass, drank deeply, then leaned forward in his chair. "Well—you've certainly spun me a fine tale, Miss Beaumont," he said, each silkily insolent word dropping like acid into her ears. "Leaving as much out as you've put in."

Feeling in need of Dutch courage before she could answer, she took a slug of Scotch and coughed and spluttered for the second time. A loud bark of laughter greeted her predicament. "Next time I catch a trespasser, remind me to pick on someone who can hold her drink."

She picked up on his change of tone. "So—I've been demoted from burglar to trespasser, have I? Presumably that means you accept that I meant no harm by entering your house."

"The British legal system is a complete mystery to me, Miss Beaumont. I'll let the friendly bobby at the local station sort out the finer details."

She licked suddenly dry lips as she contemplated the embarrassment to her family if he were to put in a complaint against her. "I see no reason for involving the police," she said stiffly. "I might have been foolish, but my intentions were entirely innocent."

"We'll let the authorities be the judge of that."

His gaze lowered as he contemplated the back of his hands with studied indifference, and it was then that Kathryn noticed the ghost of a smile hovering about his lips. Was this man just out to play games with her? Suddenly she felt certain that he had no intention of taking matters further, and never had—that he had been pulling her strings for his own warped amusement. It was time to call his bluff.

She rose and faced him. "I don't think I'll stay and participate in this ridiculous charade any longer,

Mr. Fitzalan. I've answered your questions, and as far as I'm concerned I'm free to go." He continued to watch her, no discernible expression in his slanting gray eyes.

His silence was unsettling, and she jerked her left hand up to her damp forehead to brush away errant curls, wondering uneasily why he was staring so fixedly at her arm. She looked down and he took the opportunity to vault out of his chair, striding swiftly to her side before she realized what was happening.

"You're hurt," he murmured, taking her left elbow gently in both hands.

Hurt? Bemused, she looked at her elbow, which was grazed and bleeding slightly where she had made unwilling contact with the tiled floor. It wasn't troubling her, but his nearness and touch was, as he traced a delicate pattern with one gentle finger around the edges of the red weal that marred her skin.

"It will bruise tomorrow," he murmured, his lips brushing against her temple.

He makes the words sound positively indecent, Kathryn thought, her eyelids lowering as the gentle pressure of his finger prompted a myriad of sensations. Her nerve endings tingled and her heart hammered out an unsteady rhythm. She didn't want this exquisite pleasure to stop, but reason told her that it must, and she pulled away sharply. She ignored his interrogative "Kathryn?" as she turned to collect her jacket from the arm of the chair.

She began to cross the cluttered kitchen without a backward glance, intent on getting to the entrance hall without delay.

"The front door's locked."

She was stopped in her tracks and waited, without turning.

"If you wait a moment, I'll get the key. Then you can leave in a civilized fashion." How cool he sounded, as though that brief, telling moment between them had never happened.

She heard him pulling out a drawer in the huge pine dresser, then continued on her way, aware of the steady rhythm of his footsteps behind her.

She reached the heavy oak door with relief and stepped aside as he fitted the large key in the lock, turned it, and pulled the door open.

"Good night, Kathryn." He leaned against the door jamb, arms folded across his chest, his bulk partially blocking the threshold.

Kathryn squeezed past him, the hairs on the back of her neck rising in response to their fleeting contact. Once outside, her senses steadied. Sobered by relief and the dank October air, she was able to bid him farewell in a voice that sounded unnaturally calm and quite alien to her. Then, lifting her head high, she began to walk down the drive without a backward glance, mentally congratulating herself on having escaped with some dignity intact—and without repercussions. He knew nothing about her except her name, and she wasn't even in the phone book!

As she turned the bend in the driveway a tangle of dark, interwoven conifers hid her from view and she gave in to instinct, running like a champion sprinter off the block, arriving at the stables minutes later to collapse in a heap against the gatepost.

The main house was in darkness—good. Aunt Jean usually usually went to bed early when Uncle Harry and David were away, and with any luck, no one would ever know of tonight's fiasco.

She was just crossing the yard to reach her mews flat when a whinny pulled her up short. Jasper! She'd hardly seen her own horse since she'd returned. "Hello, old thing," she said, moving up close to the handsome bay in the end box. She curled her fingers through his halter and laid her cheek against his, comforted by the warmth of his coat and his distinctive scent.

She looked around the stableyard, lit up by security lights. Hollinswood Stables had been her refuge for twenty years, ever since Jean, her mother's sister, had brought her into the warm, loving Robertson family after the car crash that left her orphaned and traumatized at the age of five. She owed her family everything. And now . . . she feared for their future.

Her mind picked reluctantly over the events set in motion by the death of Lady Alice Cardew four months ago. Eccentric but fairminded, she had refused to run the Manor estate on purely commercial lines, choosing to rent out thirty acres of prime grazing land to Hollinswood Stables for a low return simply because she was fond of Harry and Jean. Cardew lawyers, however, had not allowed her generosity to stretch beyond the grave, and insisted on a contract that terminated the Robertsons' grazing rights six months after Lady Alice's death.

Thus her death had brought business fears as well as personal grief to Kathryn and her family, but their panic eased when the new heir, a Cardew nephew, had shown himself sympathetic to their plight.

At this time of renewed optimism, Kathryn had set out on her painting trip to the South of France. News from home had been sporadic, and she had returned today to find a smoking bomb awaiting her in the news that the Manor estate had been unexpectedly sold off to some faceless corporation.

Which was no longer faceless. . . . She cursed her foolhardiness, which had led her head first into trouble. She'd only wanted to see inside the Manor in order to find out what sort of people they'd be dealing with, but she'd found out more than she'd bargained for. She winced inwardly, thrusting all thoughts of the night's events from her mind as Jasper, sensing her distress, jigged his head up and down, ears flattening. She soothed him with a soft, stroking movement to his muzzle, then, with a final hug, moved away.

As she trod wearily up the stone steps leading to her front door, exhaustion washed over her, and after going in, she went straight to her bedroom, where she undressed quickly and curled up into a tight ball under her duvet.

An hour later she switched on her bedside light, plumped up a pillow, and sat with her arms wrapped around it, her chin resting on top. She would have no rest until she confronted the most unsettling aspect of the evening.

She had found Gerard Fitzalan overbearing and highhanded, but she had to admit—reluctantly—that she found him disturbingly attractive.

But remember the past, her heart whispered. Wasn't Vincente just such a man? He had dazzled her during her final year at art college, and she had given her love to him, profoundly moved that such a worldly, self-confident man should choose her.

He had left her with a diamond ring and a promise to send for her once he had spoken to his family in Spain. She had never heard from him again, but a mutual friend had put her wise. Vincente had returned home in order to marry the daughter of a family friend, an advantageous match that was tantamount to a company merger.

Heartbroken, she had resolved to sell the diamond ring and donate the money to charity only to find the gimcrack solitaire as counterfeit as his professed love.

Since then men had been off the agenda. Art was her passion in life and developing her career as a painter her sole objective. She accepted casual dates from time to time, but no one had come close to breaching the barrier she'd thrown around herself. Until tonight . . .

The disturbing thoughts returned—had she imagined the potent attraction that had flared so tantalizingly between them?

Stop it, she told herself irritably. The whole thing's a product of overstrung nerves—nothing more. Learn from experience, unless you want to be hurt again. Perhaps Aunt Jean was right, she mused; she was always telling her to date more. If she'd had a boyfriend, she would have been immune to the tricks of someone like Gerard Fitzalan.

Yes, that's what she'd do, be more amenable to the sort of young men who frequently asked her out to dinner or to local functions. She'd choose someone kindly and reliable.

Feeling less tense, she settled herself down,

thumping her pillow in an effort to dispel unwanted thoughts before drifting into an uneasy sleep.

Chapter Two

The shrill tones of the alarm shattered Kathryn's dreams at six-thirty. She climbed reluctantly out of bed, but a hot shower tingled her skin and wakened her sluggish senses. Automatically she dressed in breeches and a sweater, made her usual breakfast of tea and toast, then took it to the long, multipaned window overlooking the stableyard. Curling up in the window seat set deep into the gritstone walls, she mulled over the practical details of morning stables.

Uncle Harry and David weren't expected back from the horse fair until midmorning; the girls would be understaffed and need help. Mentally she prioritized the tasks at hand until a glance at her watch sent her scuttling to the door, hugging her mug of tea close to her as she stepped out into the murk of an autumn morning.

She would need to see to the stabled horses first and could hear them shifting restlessly in the main block as she measured out feed and protein supplement. She hurried on her rounds, tying each animal up and replenishing food troughs and hay nets. Jasper was left to last but she gave him a loving hug before returning to the first horse, a black hunter called Sebastian, to begin cleaning out the stalls.

"Kathryn! Hi—great to see you. How was France?"

Startled, Kathryn looked up to see Cynthia, the head groom, peering down at her. Straightening up wearily she pushed stray curls back from her flushed face. "Sunny, stimulating—and full of tourists."

"Glad to be home, eh?"

"Yes, I am," Kathryn agreed. "I missed these handsome beasts." She slapped Sebastian playfully on the flank as he continued to eat, ignoring her.

"It's good of you to leap into harness on your first day back."

"Well, I knew you were shortstaffed. Thought I'd better lend a hand."

Cynthia raised an eyebrow. "Shortstaffed? Not us. Harry arranged help before he left. We've hired a couple of our old pupils for a few days. They're down at the paddocks. Tell you what, I'll take over here and you can see to Jasper. He's really missed you—we were a very poor second."

A smile wreathed Kathryn's face as she threw

down her brush and shovel and hurried to Jasper's box. Grooming her own horse was a daily pleasure, a reflective time when she mulled over problems and made decisions, often talking aloud, as though Jasper understood every word!

The fears that gnawed at her now, however, were too raw to be voiced aloud. Back home and back in the stables she could only think of one thing—their precarious business position.

With forty horses to cater for and only ten acres of their own, Manor land was essential to their viability. Without it they would have to sell some of their beloved horses, or possibly go out of business altogether. Then what would happen to the Robertsons? Especially Harry. Her fingers curled tighter round the dandy brush, and Jasper's coat received a particularly vigorous grooming as she considered her uncle's health. His arthritis was progressively disabling him; stress could only worsen his condition. Would Gerard Fitzalan, with his world-weary, cynical air and big-business mentality, take that into account when he considered their future? She feared not—he'd shown scant sympathy to her!

She was cleaning Jasper's hooves when she heard the horse box drive slowly into the yard. Uncle Harry and David! She threw the hoof pick to one side and hurried out into the sluggish October sunshine.

David was climbing down from the cab and was

just about to go to his father's aid when he saw Kathryn. With a whoop he seized her by the waist and swung her around, his blue eyes dancing. "You're back!" He set her down on her feet and held her at arm's length, eyes critical. "We nearly sent out a search party for you! You look marvellous, Kath. It must have been a great trip."

"Tell us over coffee, lass." Harry was climbing down from the passenger seat and Kathryn moved to help him, providing support until he was steady on his legs, then reaching into the cab to retrieve his stick, glad of the opportunity to avert her face. She was shocked by the change in him. New lines fanned out from his eyes, and his mouth was a thin slash in a face tightened by pain.

He swept her into a bear hug with the same old vigor, though, and she had to beg to be released—in order to breathe.

He complied, chuckling. "Time we were getting inside, anyway, love. Jean'll have the coffee waiting. Saw the curtains twitch as soon as we arrived." He began to stump toward the house. "Don't hang about, you two."

David went to follow but Kathryn pulled him back. "He looks dreadful," she muttered. "He's deteriorated so much since I saw him last, and I've only been away a few months."

"I know, love." David looked at her stricken face, thrusting his fingers through his mop of unruly blond hair in a telling gesture. "But he refuses to slow down, works all hours, and wonders why his arthritis gets worse!"

"Well, I'm back now." Kathryn hooked her arm through her cousin's as they began to cross the yard. "And I'm going to make sure I take some of the burden off his shoulders."

"Good luck, Kath." David's smile was skeptical as he entered the house, automatically stooping to avoid the low stone lintel. "You'll need it."

Over coffee and homemade biscuits they discussed Kathryn's trip, and it wasn't until there was a lull in the conversation that she had a chance to ask after their luck at the horse fair.

"No luck." Harry's large hand fisted over a biscuit. "The prices were steep. I'm not paying over the odds at the moment. Not the way things are. . . ."

The silence was overlong. Kathryn was unwilling to broach a subject she was still trying to thrust from her mind.

"I told Kathryn about the sale of the Manor," Jean said, her anxious eyes fixed on her husband.

Harry turned to his niece with a grimace. "Grand homecoming, eh, lass?" Kathryn agreed, coloring slightly.

"I wish we knew what the new owner intended to do with the place," David put in. "All we know about the guy is that he runs a telecommunications company."

"Tele-what?" Harry queried. "Isn't that just a fancy name for telephones? Pity he doesn't know how to use them. We've had no contact with the new owner at all, and there's no one at the Manor but workmen."

"We shouldn't be going up there cap in hand," David protested. "We should engage a lawyer to negotiate for us."

Next moment hot words were being exchanged in an argument Kathryn had heard before. David believed they should be seeking legal advice while Harry, characteristically, refused to "pay good money to a bunch of tight-lipped bloodsuckers."

Kathryn moved to the side to refill her cup from the coffee machine, her cheeks as heated as the scalding hot liquid. She really ought to tell the family that the new owner was at the Manor but somehow she couldn't find the words.

"What are you doing with yourself now you're back, lass?" Uncle Harry's booming voice scattered her thoughts as she turned to face three smiling faces. Once the air was cleared, peace was usually restored quickly at the Robertsons', and Kathryn rejoined them at the table with a relieved smile.

"My portfolios are bursting," she told them, "mainly with paintings of the Riviera. I'll have to trawl through and select the best ones for framing. Then they go to my outlets and then"—she raised her slim shoulders in a wry shrug—"the money starts pouring in!"

"I'm sure they'll sell well," said Jean loyally.

"So—you'll be closeted in that studio of yours, love." Harry reached for the last biscuit. "We'll not see much of you."

"I'll still help in the stables," Kathryn assured him. "I'll make the time."

"Not to worry." Harry dismissed her offer with a wave of his hand. "We can manage—and you've got your career to think of."

Kathryn and David exchanged telling glances as Harry drained his mug and pulled himself to his feet, using the chair back as a support. "I'd better go and check on the horses," he said, wheezing a little with the effort. "Can't sit here all day."

He limped from the room, but as David rose to follow Kathryn restrained him with a hand on his arm. "Don't go yet," she pleaded, "What's the latest—or rather, who's the latest? How's the love life?"

"Overactive," snorted Jean, as she began to clear the cups. "If he bottled the secret of his success he'd make a fortune."

"I'm intrigued." Kathryn shot her cousin a teasing glance.

"Slander," declared David in mock injury, hand on heart. "Tell you what, Kath, we'll go out for a drink tonight. Catch up on news. See you both later." He left with a cheery wave, leaving Kathryn and her aunt to a loaded silence.

"Don't," said Kathryn, as she bent over the task of wiping the now empty table.

"Don't do what?" remarked Jean innocently.

"You know," Kathryn muttered. "Make mental comparisons between my love life and David's."

"I could contrast your love life with David's." Jean pointed out bluntly, "but I couldn't compare it. You don't have one."

"Ouch!" Refusing to be drawn into discussion, Kathryn slung the cloth to one side and beat a retreat, citing work as her excuse.

Over the next few days Kathryn spent long hours in her studio, a large airy room which had been converted from a disused hayloft. Much of her time was spent in framing a choice selection of her French paintings, a task she took seriously, seeing it as part of her craft to choose frames that enhanced rather than swamped the delicate hues of the watercolors which were her stock in trade. The silence from the Manor was deafening, and as time went by, Kathryn began to relax. No doubt jet-setting Gerard had jetted off elsewhere.

It was only when she received a visit from an excited Ken Morris, chairman of the parish council, that she found out the truth.

"The new owner of the Manor," he told her, "and some of his colleagues wish to meet the local community. So the parish council is hosting a reception in their honor—in the village hall tomorrow night."

Kathryn had to bite her lip, hard. The village hall, erstwhile cricket pavilion with it peeling paint and a leaking roof, was hardly the sort of venue such people would be used to.

"Parish funds will run to some wine," Ken declared proudly, "a couple of glasses each, and we can put on 'nibbles'—er, cheese and crackers, that sort of thing."

Kathryn groaned inwardly but commented politely that it sounded well under control.

"So you will come, won't you, Kathryn?"

"Me?" Kathryn had assumed she would be able to opt out. "Well—no . . . it's rather, er, short notice."

"But Kathryn, you must! Mr Fitzalan wants to meet everyone in the village, and I promised I'd do my best. As a parish council member, it's your duty."

"But I only take the minutes at meetings," Kathryn protested.

"Quite—you're an invaluable member of the

team." He took her resigned shrug as submission and issued his final orders on his way out of her apartment. "Seven o'clock sharp to help set up, Kathryn. Our guests are expected at seven-thirty."

Kathryn leaned against the closed door, fuming. Ken, in characteristic fashion, had steamrollered her; she'd have to make the best of a potentially awkward situation.

The following evening found her serving drinks from behind long trestle tables covered in white paper tablecloths, feeling like an overdressed barmaid. She had taken pains with her appearance—for her own self-esteem, she had told herself—and wore her one good suit. Well cut, in royal blue, the fitted jacket and short, pencil-slim skirt molded her curves, showing off her shapely figure and long legs. A wrapover silk blouse in oyster peeked from between the broad lapels of her jacket, and a string of antique jet beads encircled her neck, highlighting the paleness of her skin. Matching side combs pulled her hair back from her face; her hair then tumbled to her shoulders in a riot of curls. Her black shoes, very elegant with high, spiky heels, had been an impulse buy from an exclusive boutique. And hardly ever worn, she reminded herself, surreptitiously removing one of them and flexing a foot relieved to be out of its cramped confinement.

Looking around she couldn't see David or Uncle

Harry, though it was difficult to pick anyone out as most of the village seemed to be crammed into the small hall.

Kathryn collected her own drink and began to circulate, unsurprised to find her friends and neighbors expressing views that mirrored her own anxieties. How would change at the Manor affect Hollinswood's tight-knit community? Could it destroy their sleepy way of life?

She turned at the sound of Ken's voice to find three of the newcomers standing on the platform at the front of the hall. Gerard Fitzalan was flanked by a dark-suited, distinguished-looking silver-haired gentleman and by a petite blond woman clad in a close-fitting cream jersey suit offset by chunky gold jewelry. Suddenly Kathryn felt like a dowdily dressed beanpole.

Her eyes were drawn irresistibly to the tall central figure. Strange to see Gerard in his clothes, she thought wickedly, noting the casual elegance of his taupe suit, ivory-colored shirt, and loosely knotted brown tie. A hush descended as he spoke, introducing the other man as Douglas Talbot, his chief executive, and the woman as Sarah Vine, his personal assistant.

"Wow! Wonder what she personally assists him with?"

Kathryn turned to find David had stolen up on her. "Take a cold shower," she hissed back, smiling.

She turned to listen as Gerard thanked Ken for organizing the reception. Then, preamble over, he stepped forward, his keen gray eyes scanning the company as though taking the measure of a potentially critical audience. His angular features broke unexpectedly into a warm smile, and Kathryn couldn't help a sudden leap of her pulse, uneasily aware of a potent charisma at work as he broke the silence.

"I promise to be brief, but I must say how delighted we are at Fitzalan Enterprises to be joining you in such a beautiful and tranquil part of the world." He paused for breath, or effect, his melodious voice deepening as though he was now coming to the main point of his speech. "It was these assets that persuaded us to select the Manor as our new European headquarters." As if sensing a sudden disquiet, he held one hand up in a placatory gesture. "That does not mean that the Manor will become an office block. In sad disrepair at the moment, it will be restored sympathetically, doing full justice to one of the finest examples of domestic Jacobean architecture in the country." Murmurs of approval greeted this announcement but Kathryn shifted restlessly from one foot to the other. All well and good, she wanted to shout out, but what about the land? What happens to that?

Her mental cry unanswered, Gerard Fitzalan continued. "We will be creating jobs—many that provide positions and training for young people—and I will make it my personal responsibility to ensure that as many staff members as possible are recruited locally." An excited buzz greeted this news and Kathryn looked from the keen faces around her to the face of the man who seemed able to manipulate an audience with a few well-chosen words. "My company will work closely with the local community to ensure we bring benefit, not blight," he went on, driving home his point. "And . . ." He raised a glass of champagne Ken handed to him, his eyes as clear and bright as the sparkling liquid. "I propose a toast. To the long and fruitful association between Fitzalan Enterprises and Hollinswood village!"

Applause, and not a little relief, greeted these words, and Kathryn drained her own glass in one nervous movement, barely noticing the taste or flavor. Gerard Fitzalan might be a master of public relations, but was he sincere? And, if not, what would be the consequences for her own family?

She felt stifled by the heat and turned to leave only to find herself pushed up against the wall as people surged forward to renew their refreshments. As the crowd thinned she made another attempt to reach the exit and was making good progress when she found herself facing Ken Morris.

"Kathryn!" He held on to her arm, barring her way as she turned to find Gerard Fitzalan before her.

Ken's introduction was cheery. "Mr. Fitzalan—Kathryn Beaumont. Kathryn's a neighbor of yours. She lives—"

"Nearby," put in Kathryn.

"To be sure," Ken said vaguely as Kathryn's hand was enveloped by a much larger one.

"Delighted," Gerard drawled. "Always pleased to meet a neighbor. Feel free to *drop in* anytime."

To Kathryn's annoyance, color flooded her cheeks, while Ken smiled benignly from one to the other.

"Tell me, Miss Beaumont," Gerard continued as his grip tightened on her hand. "What line of work are you in? Something *enterprising* I'm sure."

"I'm a freelance artist," Kathryn said shortly, making a vain attempt to tug her hand away.

Gerard's brows lifted. "Indeed? That's just the sort of profession I would expect you to *enter.*"

"Kathryn's one of our local stars," Ken added.

"I'm sure she's a woman of many talents," Gerard murmured, a soft light kindling his gray eyes.

Goodness, she'd pass out soon if she didn't escape this hothouse—and this man with his embarrassing allusions! Gerard now had both hands holding hers, and short of kicking him in the shins, she didn't know how to free herself.

"Gerard! There you are." One small tanned hand curled around Gerard's arm, and Sarah's gilt head leaned briefly against his shoulder before she raised her eyes to his. "There are people over here simply dying to meet you."

Gerard's hands fell instantly from Kathryn's, and with a dismissive nod he was gone, Ken following in his wake.

Kathryn flexed her hand, relieved to be free of the bone-crushing handshake but not too keen on the method used. She glanced balefully at Sarah's retreating back.

It really was time to leave, but as she turned she was pounced on by a friend wanting to know all about her recent trip.

It was a full twenty minutes before she escaped, flinging the exit door open with relief, her heels tapping a tattoo on the wooden deck as she crossed the veranda. She felt the need to cool down before facing the walk home and perched on the wooden balustrade, stretching her long legs out in front of her. It was no wonder she felt wound up after the awkward encounter inside when, with Ken looking on, she'd had to stand there like a dummy, greeting Gerard's insolence with polite endurance. She slid one hand beneath her hair and lifted the heavy tresses, enjoying the gentle play of the breeze on the back of her neck as her eyelids lowered.

"Kathryn! There you are!"

Kathryn's eyes snapped open as she almost lost

her balance, clutching at the balustrade to right herself.

Gerard Fitzalan was advancing toward her, shrouded in evening gloom, the wooden deck reverberating to the beat of his tread. Instinctively she shifted position, her jacket slipping unnoticed from her lap, until she found herself backed up against the side wall of the veranda, a flickering lamp above her head bathing her in anemic light.

"Why did you leave the other night without telling me where I could find you?" Gerard's tall figure loomed over her, shadows masking his face.

"You threatened me with the police—I wasn't going to leave a forwarding address!"

His hands rose, palms outward. "Just my little joke, Kate."

Joke! It had been no laughing matter to her! With one deft movement he sat on the balustrade, his right knee making close contact with her thigh as he turned toward her.

"Ready to do another runner, Kate? What are you so keen to run from, I wonder."

"Overbearing, sarcastic men," she snapped, "with no manners and no inclination to acquire them!"

To her fury, a deep-throated chuckle greeted her litany of insults. "I'm glad I've made such a strong impression—on so short an acquaintance."

Really! He twisted everything around to suit himself, but in one respect he was right, she was over-reacting—and she didn't know why. All she did know was that it was time to leave and—

"You're doing it again, Kate."

"Doing what?" Was he a mind reader now?

"Planning a hasty exit," he explained, his mouth twisting into a wry smile. "I call that very ungrateful, after all the trouble I've taken to find you."

Gerard looking for her? Surely not. Still—when the dish of the day was a blonde, a redhead might appear an appetizing side dish.

"You shouldn't have bothered!" She immediately regretted her childish retort, but he seized on it with relish, his reply laced with quiet menace.

"Oh, but I should. You see—there's unfinished business between us."

"There's nothing between us," Kathryn returned, "and never will be." In the heart-stopping moment that followed, she was suddenly aware of the black flecks that marbled his gray irises as he slanted her a glance as dark as Lucifer.

"Is that a challenge?"

"No—I . . . well . . ." She cursed her leaden tongue, color flooding her cheeks as she focused her defiance into a wide, antagonistic stare.

He exhaled abruptly, as though her venom had found its target, then leaned forward, coiling one long forefinger into a corkscrrew curl. "Don't fight it, Kate."

Fight what? What on earth was he talking about? She opened her lips to emit some acid rejoinder, and found herself saying, "No one calls me Kate."

"Except me," he corrected. "That's something we alone will share. Together with other good things."

The look in his eyes should have forewarned her but she was taken completely by surprise when his arms coiled around her like steel bands and she was tilted into the crook of his arm, her hair cascading like a russet waterfall as his face moved triumphantly above hers. Words of protest died on her lips as his mouth claimed hers, her senses swimming as the gentle caress became more demanding and she found herself responding as though she had no will of her own.

"Gerard?" The imperious voice punctured her dream as Gerard released her so abruptly that she almost slipped to the floor. He stood up, blocking her from view, as he turned to face Douglas Talbot.

"I think it might be politic to return to the reception now." Talbot's perfectly modulated tones held a subtle warning, but what astonished Kathryn was Gerard's ready compliance. With a quick nod in her direction, he was gone, rejoining the chattering throng revealed by the open doorway, slamming the door shut to leave Kathryn alone on the veranda.

She hugged herself, teeth chattering, not knowing whether she was trembling from rage or cold—or both. Slipping on her jacket made her feel a little warmer, and she set her face for home, almost tripping as she hurried down the veranda steps.

It was uphill all the way and her shoes were uncomfortable, but she made good progress, indignation firing her heels. Gerard had dumped her like unwanted garbage as soon as his classy friend had turned up! Furiously she kicked at a large pebble and instantly regretted the impulse as pain seared through an already suffering foot. Blast this expensive footwear! She took the shoe off and, balancing on one leg, rubbed her chafed foot, almost falling over as the glare of headlights robbed her momentarily of sight.

A limousine almost the width of the entire lane purred to a halt beside her, causing her to hobble up against the stone wall, her shoe held defensively before her. She'd accept no lift; she'd be darned if she'd get in.

The driver's door opened and a chauffeur in a blue-gray uniform walked around the front of the car toward her. He looks like an actor in a costume drama, she thought, her tense mood threatening to transmute into giggles. Then she saw what he was holding out—her woolly hat, bedraggled and scruffy-looking. Silently she took it from him, and with a brief salute he returned to the car to bring the engine to life.

There was movement in the back seat as the car

roared off into the dark. In spite of the shaded glass there was no mistaking that gilded head—Sarah Vine! Gerard must be there as well, most likely laughing at her!

A few moments later she reached the stables and slung the hat onto the manure heap as she stomped through the yard. No point in wasting good compost.

Her apartment felt cheerless so she went straight to bed, wrapped in a capacious dressing gown that made her feel like a candlewick tent. No matter— it was shapeless, and just about matched her mood!

The next morning, pale sunbeams, filtered through threadbare chintz curtains, fingered her face to wakefulness. With a jolt she realized it was nine-thirty, and she moved quickly into her kitchen to prepare a meager breakfast. After eating she went for her shower, relieved to discard the dressing gown, and luxuriated beneath needle points of steaming hot water.

After dressing in working clothes, she had just begun to towel-dry her hair when the doorbell rang. Who on earth would call at this time?

She hurried to the door, words of greeting dying on her lips as the door swung open to reveal Gerard Fitzalan, his auburn, spiky hair tousled by the wind and a broad smile on his face.

Chapter Three

"How did you find out where I live?" Instantly Kathryn wanted to bite back her gauche, clumsy words. Why, oh why, did her social skills disappear as soon as this man appeared on the scene?

"Morning, Kathryn," Gerard said pointedly, his mouth set in a suspiciously straight line. "I spoke to your uncle last night and he revealed your secret hideaway."

His eyes followed the hot pulse of blood rising in her cheeks as Kathryn pulled nervous fingers through her damp curls. "As you can see, it's not convenient—"

"Only Mrs. Robertson thought you could help me."

"In what way?" Kathryn asked blankly.

"By finding me a suitable mount," he explained. "I want to ride while I'm in the area. Harry told me to drop by this morning, and Mrs. Robertson has sent me up here."

"You're experienced, I presume?"

"Very."

Ignoring his wickedly suggestive tone, Kathryn glanced toward the main house, sensing her aunt's presence behind the net curtains. What on earth was Jean up to? Looking balefully at Gerard she felt a strong desire to slam the door in his face and wipe away his smug grin, but business for the stables must come first. She had no option but to play hostess.

"Come in," she said a little ungraciously, standing away from the doorway. Gerard ducked to avoid the low lintel, then entered, striding into the center of the room. Placing his hands on his denim-clad hips, he began to direct sharp glances into every corner of her rectangular, low-ceilinged living room with its exposed beams of pale, coarse oak.

Watching him, Kathryn found herself seeing her living space through a stranger's eyes and wondered what he made of the eclectic mix of furnishings rehabilitated from junk shops and the large floor cushions in brightly patterned covers strewn around the sanded wooden floor.

She felt as though every aspect of her life was up for scrutiny, and when he jerked his head in her direction and said, "This is just the sort of room I imagined you in, Kate—original and colorful," she felt no reassurance, only blind panic that he should be thinking of her at all!

She thanked him for what she assumed was a compliment but Gerard cut into her mumbling. "I'm sorry I didn't see you again after Douglas surprised us last night." Annoyance must have flashed across her features, for he turned to face her, concern shadowing his eyes. "I didn't like leaving you alone on the veranda, Kathryn, but I wanted to bundle Douglas away before he or anyone else saw whom I was with. I know what small communities can be like, and the last thing I wanted was for you to become the victim of vulgar gossip."

Or himself, she decided churlishly—but it was an explanation of sorts and she stammered out an appropriate reply, her dampened hands twisting the thick fabric of her sweater as unwelcome images of what had occurred on the veranda darted into her head.

Awareness fleeted across his face, the firm lips quirking at the corners as he continued in the same placatory tone. "When I knew I wouldn't be able to get away, I sent the car after you to take you home—but Sarah said they were unable to find you."

So, it was Sarah who'd organized the charade with the hat! "Well, thanks for the thought," said Kathryn, trying to imbue her tone with some warmth. "If you'll excuse me one moment, I'll just finish drying my hair."

She darted into her bedroom, thankful for a moment alone to mull over what Gerard had said. His words had put his behavior into a different light, but was she being naive in taking them at face value? Aside from her personal relations with Gerard, which seemed complicated enough—what exactly had he and Uncle Harry discussed during their cosy chat? Had the question of their grazing lands come up?

She longed to know but caution told her it would be unwise to tackle Gerard on a subject that was so close to her heart. Her instincts told her that it would be foolish to reveal vulnerability around this man.

She brushed through her hair one last time, tied it at the nape of her neck with a purple ribbon, and returned to find Gerard surveying the prints and paintings dotted along the rear whitewashed wall of her living room.

"Are any of these yours?" he queried.

"All of the water colors," she admitted, feeling uncharacteristically nervous as he contemplated them in silence. She had never lacked confidence in her work before, and although she was self-critical, using her personal best as a yardstick, she never doubted her innate ability. Now she breathlessly awaited Gerard's judgment.

"They're exquisite," he said, and Kathryn exhaled, surprised at the keen pleasure his words brought. "You have great gifts, Kathryn Beaumont."

She moved closer, drawn irresistibly to his side by the strength of his approval. "You transmute harsh upland scenery into symphonies of light and shade. You highlight the beauty but take away the danger. Is that wise?" His mesmeric silver eyes slanted down at her, and Kathryn blinked in an effort to break the connection, bewildered by the turn the conversation was taking.

"Isn't danger necessary—and exciting?" he continued, his velvet-soft voice acting as a link between them as Kathryn struggled to regain control of the situation.

"For a while," she said musingly, amazed that her cool tones did not betray her inner agitation, "but the novelty soon palls."

His angular features tightened a fraction. Then he returned his gaze to the wall.

A smile hovered about Kathryn's lips as she realized she'd just riposted one of Gerard's clever lines and, newly confident, turned from him with brisk words. "I think we have a suitable mount if you'd like to come with me please." Without waiting for a reply she led the way down to the yard and through to Sebastian's loose box.

The hunter was in a particularly spiky mood and

flattened his ears on their approach, moving restlessly from side to side. Kathryn glanced from Sebastian, seventeen hands of well-muscled stallion, to Gerard who stood, arms akimbo and legs apart, taking his measure. She had been right; it was a match made in heaven.

"He's a handsome brute," Gerard stated, eyes alight.

"Brute's the word," Kathryn agreed. "When he's in one of his awkward moods he'll try every trick in the book to unseat the rider. A lot of experienced people have come unstuck—believe me."

"Are you issuing a challenge?" He darted a sidelong glance at her.

"Certainly not," she protested. "I don't play games with safety. I'm issuing a warning—make sure he knows who's boss right from the start."

"I will," stated Gerard. Then he added, "Perhaps you should chaperone me on my first ride as you're concerned for my safety."

That had not been Kathryn's intention and she was just about to say so when Cynthia's head appeared around the open door of the loose box. "Hi, Kathryn. Thought I heard someone in here and assumed it was you and—" Blatantly her eyes tracked up and down Gerard's athletic figure and came to rest on his face. For one dreadful moment Kathryn thought Cynthia was going to wolf-whistle, so she rushed in with introductions, reflecting wryly on the effect Gerard had on women as he gave Cynthia's hand a friendly shake.

"Pleased to meet you, Mr. Fitzalan." Cynthia dimpled, then turned back to Kathryn as though in afterthought. "I brought Jasper in from the paddocks. That's what I've come to tell you."

"Is that your horse, Kathryn?" Gerard asked. When she nodded, he went on with, "Since we both have mounts, why not go out right now? I'm anxious to try Sebastian as soon as possible." He looked disdainfully at his denims. "I'm not properly dressed but it won't matter for once. I assume you have a hard hat I can borrow?"

"Of course, Cynthia will fix you up. But I don't think I can go. I . . . have a lot of work to do," Kathryn temporized.

"Lame excuse, Kate," countered Gerard. "Think how well you'll work after you've felt the wind in your hair and feasted your eyes on beautiful scenery." When she didn't reply, he turned to Cynthia with a rueful smile. "The woman has no soul. . . ."

"All right," Kathryn conceded, shortly. Really, the presence of Cynthia who was hanging open-mouthed on every word made it very difficult to refuse, especially when the stables needed the business so much. "I'll go and saddle up Jasper. Perhaps you can help Cynthia with Sebastian?"

"Of course." He flashed Cynthia a brilliant smile, which sent her scurrying to the tack room.

When Kathryn led Jasper into the yard, she found Gerard alone with Sebastian checking the tightness of his saddle's girth. He watched Jasper approach with the eye of an experienced horseman.

"He's beautiful, Kate," he said, his smile reaching into the far corners of his eyes. "Well proportioned, with a neat head."

"Thank you," said Kathryn, blushing with pleasure. "Jasper was sired here," she told him as she mounted, "and I schooled him myself, just before I left to study art. We've always made a great team."

As soon as Gerard mounted Sebastian Kathryn realized, with relief, that he would be able to handle the temperamental animal. They set off and, wishing to avoid the road altogether, Kathryn led Gerard through the paddocks and on to the bridle path that ran through the local woods.

"You ride extremely well. Were you born in the saddle?" Kathryn gave abrupt voice to her curiosity as the trees enclosed them and the sound of the horses' hooves became muffled by layers of decaying leaf litter.

"Hardly," he answered drily. "I was born in New York City. Fat gray pigeons were the only wildlife I saw until I was seven."

"And what happened then?" she prompted.

"Dad inherited the family estate at Connemara. We returned to the Old Country, and I was brought up there. I returned to New York when I began working for the family firm, but I've never forgotten my rural roots."

Of course, an Irish connection! That explained the lilt that flavored his mid-Atlantic tones. Lost in thought she almost missed his next words, until their significance sank in. "Pardon?" she said shortly.

"I was just pointing out," he went on patiently, "that our early experiences are similar. You were born in London and moved to the country when you were young."

"When I was orphaned," Kathryn confirmed, "but how on earth . . . ?"

"Your uncle told me last night. He's proud of his talented niece and likes to talk about you."

Kathryn digested this information in silence.

"Did you go to art college in London in order to rediscover your roots?" Gerard asked, enjoying the effect of his broadside as Kathryn's head swung round to his.

"Good heavens, did you get my full biography from Uncle Harry?"

"Some of it," he chuckled. "At least what was suitable for public consumption."

Color stained Kathryn's cheeks as she tried to think what her garrulous relative could have disclosed! To deflect further probing she answered his original question. "I didn't return to London to search out my roots, as it happens. Early life with my parents lives on in my memory, and I've never felt the need to revisit childhood haunts. I chose London for practical reasons. I wanted to get a degree in Fine Arts and the city offered the best courses."

"But you returned to Hollinswood when you'd finished?"

"The day after I graduated," Kathryn admitted. "Metropolitan life wasn't really for me, and living at home meant I could pursue my dream of a freelance career. Without my family's support," she told him soberly, "I'd be teaching by day while dreaming and painting by night." Which still might happen if this man, riding quietly by her side, did anything to injure the family business, Kathryn thought forlornly. Not wanting to dwell on that unpleasant prospect she attempted to change the subject. "Do your parents still live in Connemara?"

"My mother does. Dad died five years ago." Gerard's eyes turned aside to peer into a thicket of tangled bushes, his jaw tightening.

"I'm sorry . . . I didn't know."

"No reason why you should." Gerard pulled Sebastian up, lifted up a large oak branch that was blocking their way, and held it steady while Kathryn passed by. "We've adjusted," he continued, urging his mount on as the branch snapped shut behind them. "Mother's a feisty New Yorker. She threw herself into running the family estate, and I have my hands full with Fitzalan Enterprises. I took over when Dad died—in my mid-twenties."

"Did your father start the company?"

"He certainly did. He began as a newspaperman, bought an ailing business on the East Coast of America, and ended up with a chain! He was a formidable operator. When we moved to Ireland he commuted across the Atlantic weekly to keep our Stateside business afloat. In time he diversified into telecommunications, and Fitzalan Enterprises was born."

His voice was shot through with pride, and Kathryn was struck forcibly by the difference in their situations. Her meager, erratic income and modest lifestyle was a world away from corporate politics and a sophisticated, metropolitan existence. Gerard might claim to be a country boy, but the similarities between them ended there.

The path narrowed and began to run uphill as they reverted to single file, Kathryn leading. Enfolded by the trees, the quiet of the woods and the steady rhythm of the horses' hooves lulled them into a companionable silence, and it occurred to Kathryn that this was the first time she had been able to relax in this man's presence—the only time in their short acquaintance in which he had not set out to rattle her.

They took a sharp incline to the right as the trees began to thin out and the terrain grew bleaker. The horses' breathing was becoming labored when Kathryn pulled up and turned in the saddle. "Wait for it. Surprise corner." She tugged on Jasper's right rein, urged him on through two huge, upended boulders forming a natural archway, then disappeared from Gerard's view.

Gerard followed suit to find Kathryn waiting for him, her face lit by a broad smile. "And this is the surprise."

They were high up on a broad, open plateau, with dramatic views on all sides. It was as though the hilltop had been sliced through by a sharp knife and covered by a flat grassy paddock. In spite of the dour, gray day, they could see for miles—drystone walls, like rows of broken, jagged teeth, dissected a hummocky green landscape dotted by the white shapes of grazing sheep and studded by huge outcrops of millstone grit.

"There's the village." Kathryn pointed in a south easterly direction toward a collection of pewter-colored buildings with steeply pitched stone roofs, huddled around the central spire of the parish church.

"It's spectacular," Gerard breathed, leaning forward in his saddle, eyes eager to pick out every detail.

"When I was a child I thought this place was the rooftop of the world," Kathryn told him. She nodded toward the grassy space stretching before them. "I enjoyed many a wild gallop across the plateau."

"Did you indeed . . . ?" Gerard's head tilted toward her, his eyes issuing a challenge.

Kathryn needed no encouragement. With a cry she urged Jasper on but her words were lost to the elements as the wind whipped around her. She rode low over Jasper, her heart pounding in time with his thudding hooves, laughter bubbling to her lips as exhilaration took hold of her.

The two horses were keeping pace, the raw competitiveness alive between animals and riders, but as the end of the plateau came into view, the superior muscle power of the hunter began to show, and Sebastian edged forward.

Before he could get a head in front they came to a shuddering halt, horses sweating, their flanks heaving. "My win, I think," claimed Gerard, dismounting nimbly. He removed his headgear with signs of relief, dropping the hat casually onto the springy turf before moving to Kathryn's side, where she sat astride Jasper, trying to catch her breath.

"Rubbish. A draw!" Laughing, Kathryn removed her hard hat, shaking out her tangled curls before drawing one leg over the saddle and sliding into Gerard's waiting arms.

He set her down on her feet, eyes slanting down at her as his hands brushed up her arms to rest on her shoulders. The scudding dark clouds broke rank, and a shaft of sunlight, surprisingly strong for late autumn, gilded them.

Kathryn could see threads of crimson in Gerard's dark red tresses as the sun lit him, and it reminded her of the first time they had met. Her hat fell unnoticed to her feet as her hands rose of their own volition to his forehead and, with gentle downward strokes, she began to explore the planes and contours of his face. "I wanted to do this the first moment I saw you," she explained breathlessly. "It must be the artist in me."

"I'm all for encouraging art," he murmured, his eyes closing in appreciation of her caress.

Suddenly Kathryn's hands fell, nestling on his chest, and when his eyes flicked open in protest, he found apprehension shadowing her features. "Hey— relax." His hands massaged her shoulders, kneading her soft flesh through the fine woollen sweater. "You're not doing anything wrong."

Of course she was! She didn't know what had possessed her to touch him in such a fashion, but if she didn't call a halt now, she'd be drawn into something she would regret. She must let him down gently, she decided, but as his head lowered to hers, panic knotted her hands and she pushed against his hard chest with all the strength she could muster. "No!"

The simple negative froze his features and emptied light from his eyes as his hands fell from her and he took a step back. "What have I done wrong now, Kathryn?"

She couldn't lay all the blame at his door, not after the outrageous way she'd just behaved, so she attempted a conciliatory tone. "You've done nothing wrong as such, Gerard. It's just that your approach is a little, well . . . blatant. I hardly know you and yet you expect . . ." Her words trailed away as she found herself unable to voice what he did expect.

Realization dawned on his face. "I see. I'm moving way too fast for your prissy ways."

"I've never been prissy in my life!"

"No?" He took a menacing step closer and she steeled herself to hold her ground. "Than why do you live in a quiet backwater—alone?"

"That's my choice—and my business." She forced the words out through stiffened lips, furious that he should subject her safe, cosy world to his sneering scrutiny.

"It could be mine."

Kathryn froze, disconcerted by the provocative words and change of mood which had brought a smile of devastating charm to his lean features. "If you want the more conventional approach," he went on, "we could go out to dine, go in for the sort of social chit-chat new couples enjoy. It would take an age to get to know each other, but that's the price one pays for conforming to the rules."

Kathryn was appalled by the world-weary tone of his voice, which seemed to express contempt for all the values she held dear. She knew it was time to put him straight. "I don't think there can be anything between us, Gerard, conventional or otherwise. We come from different worlds, you and I. Perhaps it's better to acknowledge that now—before we're drawn into something we might regret." She was astonished at the coolness of her tone, which belied her inner agitation, but the less Gerard knew of her mixed emotions the better.

She twisted her head away as he digested her words in silence.

"Well . . ." he said, finally. "You've made your feelings quite clear." He turned and strode away to where Sebastian was grazing. "I'll make my own way back."

He took the fragile warmth of the day with him, the sun refusing to leave the sanctuary of the iron-gray clouds as the cool air misted around her. She stood alone on the hillside.

Chapter Four

"Gerard's gone, then?"

Kathryn started on her way up to her flat and turned to face Jean's crestfallen face. "Yes," she mumbled. She had arrived back to find Sebastian in his box, munching his way through a fresh haynet. Gerard was nowhere to be seen.

"Well, I've just brought a fresh batch of scones out of the oven, so you'd better come in and eat them."

Kathryn followed reluctantly. Just now she could do without company, but seated at the table, biting into the warm, doughy scones and sipping the hot, strong tea, a familiar feeling of comfort stole over her.

"Gerard didn't stick around, then?" Jean asked curiously.

"Er . . . no," Kathryn hedged. "I daresay he had to get back to work."

"Pity," Jean commented. "I'd have liked to have seen him again. I enjoyed his company last night."

"Last night?" Kathryn queried, one eyebrow shooting up.

"Yes, love," Jean replied. "He brought Harry back when David wanted to stay on. Sat round this very table and I made us all some cocoa." Jean prattled on about how charming he'd been—"no airs and graces"—while Kathryn's thoughts raced. Gerard having a cosy tête-à-tête with her family? What on earth had they talked about? Surely not . . .

"The land," Kathryn blurted out. "Did you get a chance to ask about the land?"

The scone dropped from Jean's hand as her arms reached across the table to give her niece a quick, fierce hug. "I was going to let Harry tell you but I can't keep quiet any longer." She let go of Kathryn and leaned back, beaming. "Everything's going to be all right! We can keep using the land. Harry fixed it up with Gerard last night."

Kathryn squealed, hugging her aunt in return just as Harry entered and wanted to know what all the fuss was about.

"I told her about the land deal," Jean said, laughing and disentangling herself from Kathryn's embrace.

"Isn't it great?" Harry joined them at the table, beginning to demolish a scone even before he was seated.

"Tell me what happened," Kathryn pleaded.

"I pigeonholed Gerard last night at the reception and told him the whole sorry tale. He was very sympathetic and, to cut a long story short, he's given me his word that we can lease Manor lands in perpetuity. Fixed rent—same as we pay now. His company has no interest in the land at all—it's the house they need. I've to go and see this Douglas Talbot, fix up the formalities. This time I'll make sure we set up a cast-iron covenant!"

"Uncle Harry, I'm so pleased."

"So am I, lass so am I . . ." He let out a long, heartfelt sigh of relief, and Kathryn noticed the change the good news had already wrought in his appearance. The lines around his eyes were less pronounced, and his cheeks were softer, more filled out. Her mood swung sky-high as she contemplated their newfound security.

"Seems we've got ourselves a good landlord," Harry went on. Kathryn had to agree, color etching her cheeks as he asked, "How did you get on with him this morning? Find a suitable mount?"

"Yes, yes, I did," said Kathryn, gulping her tea. "Sebastian."

"Thought so," Harry chuckled. "I suspect the old devil's met his match in Gerard Fitzalan."

"Gerard can certainly handle him," Kathryn confirmed, glad to get on to the topic of horse talk. "And he seemed pleased with Sebastian's performance."

"Good. Might get some lucrative business out of the Manor. From what Gerard was saying, they expect to entertain a lot of business folk, mainly Europeans. May as well give them an authentic taste of English country life the hard way—on the back of a horse!"

Kathryn listened with half an ear as he talked of plans to increase stock. It was wonderful to hear him speak of the future with such confidence, now that the cloud of uncertainty had lifted. And all thanks to Gerard, who had not behaved like the hard and ruthless businessman she believed him to be. Had she misjudged him? She felt more confused than ever.

"Gerard's gone, then?" The door slammed shut behind David's entry, startling her out of her reverie. She groaned, putting her head briefly into her hands. So David had joined the Gerard Fitzalan fan club as well? She stood up, made an abrupt comment about needing to get on with work, then left, leaving puzzled faces behind her.

For the next week the family saw little of her. Her French landscapes were proving popular, and she now had to frame the next selection of pictures.

Gerard visited the stables daily to exercise Sebastian, but Kathryn's heavy workload gave her a good excuse to avoid him. Better to keep a discreet distance, she reasoned, for she still did not trust him. In brutally honest moments, she admitted to herself that she trusted her own reactions to him far less, but, either way, there was no point in tempting fate by spending too much time in his company!

After a particularly hard day Kathryn was relieved when David prised her away from her studio and took her for an early evening drink in the village pub. It was pleasant to unwind in the "Rose and Crown," warmed by a roaring log fire and a glass of red wine.

"So," David said, cradling his pint glass in his hand, "do you want to double-date or not?"

"Date?" Kathryn's head shot around. "Who?"

"Really, Kath, I could tell you weren't listening. I've just been telling you about Steve Barrington. His girl's just dumped him for some other guy. Well, he's always had a thing about you, and if we could arrange an evening out, a foursome, it would cheer him up no end."

Kathryn eyed her cousin doubtfully. "I'm not sure I'd be much good as an agony aunt."

"I don't think he'll spend all evening crying on your shoulder. But you need a break from work, and he needs taking out of himself. Could do you both some good."

Her cousin was right, and she had resolved to

make an effort to meet more men. "Okay," she agreed. "Let's fix something up. Who will you take?"

"Jenny, probably," David said vaguely.

"Good, she's nice." Jenny was a bubbly brunette who shared David's casual approach to relationships. And good luck to them, Kathryn thought forlornly—getting emotionally involved hadn't done her much good. But it was time she took a chance on love again, and agreeing to a date with an old friend was at least a beginning.

In the same optimistic frame of mind, Kathryn set out to find herself a new outfit, and in one of the more exclusive boutiques in the next town, a saleswoman, with a world-weary, sophisticated air, persuaded Kathryn to try on a figure-hugging dress in black crushed velvet. It had long sleeves and a scooped neckline, so Kathryn had initially demurred—surely the neckline was too low, and the hemline too high? But she had been soundly put in her place. With Madam's svelte figure and long legs, it would be a crime not to wear such a dress!

It had certainly impressed Steve when she opened the door. His hazel eyes lightened and brown hair flopped across his forehead as he leaned forward to kiss her and present her with a bunch of roses in a delicate shade of pink. "You look gorgeous, Kathryn, simply gorgeous."

Pleased, Kathryn collected her things and joined

the others. They piled into Steve's car, a happy jokey foursome, Kathryn in the back with Jenny, swapping gossip, while David sat in the passenger seat and gave directions.

Oakwood Hall, converted from a Victorian shooting lodge, retained the architectural details of a more luxuriant era. The reception area was paneled in dark oak, and elaborate brass sconces held wall lamps that cast discreet pools of light across crimson carpets. The host took their coats, then led them into the bar for pre-dinner drinks.

Kathryn and Jenny perched on bar stools, still chatting, while Steve and David attempted to catch the bartender's eye. Kathryn tossed her hair back in a sudden carefree gesture; she was going to enjoy herself tonight, she was sure of it.

"Why, Kathryn. How nice to see you."

Kathryn swiveled on her stool to find Gerard at her side, and she felt her heart skid as color crested her cheeks. Why, oh why, did she always behave like a schoolgirl around this man? He showed no sign of nerves, looking cool and relaxed in a charcoal gray suit, blue silk tie, and white cambric shirt, his features shadowed by the subdued lighting. Kathryn introduced her companions, and he smiled from one to the other.

"Well, ladies, you've chosen a fine restaurant. I do hope you enjoy your meal."

He's going in for that social chit-chat he despises so much, Kathryn thought wryly. Still, now that they were face to face, she must speak with him, she owed him that much. Turning to Jenny she excused herself, then slipped off her stool, drawing Gerard to one side.

"Actually," she said with studied casualness, "I've been meaning to speak to you all week."

"Really?" he said, one brow raised. "You could have fooled me. I had the distinct impression you were avoiding me."

"Oh, no, I've just been busy working. Well . . ." She forced a smile to her lips. "I just wanted to thank you for putting Uncle Harry's mind at rest. Now that he knows our lands are secure, his health's improved and he's making business plans—"

"I don't want your thanks," he cut in. "I did what I thought was right, that's all."

How cold he sounded, so distant. She shifted uneasily.

"So, if there's nothing more?" he queried.

"Not really, I . . ." She struggled to find the right words—any words. She had meant to keep him at bay, not alienate him totally, and was finding his chilly disdain difficult to handle. Involuntarily her hand reached toward him, as though attempting to breach the gap between them. His slanting gray eyes revealed nothing of his emotions, but for one infinitesimal moment he seemed to lean toward her, his harsh expression beginning to soften. "The thing is," she stammered, "the thing is . . ."

Steve chose that moment to return. His arm snaked around her waist, and he pulled Kathryn against him with all the possessiveness of a long-time boyfriend. I've known him since I was in pig-tails, she thought, yet he picks this instant to demonstrate his affection!

Surprise, swiftly controlled, fleeted across Gerard's face. Kathryn barely had time to mumble brief introductions before Gerard turned away, his long strides taking him to a darkened corner of the room.

It was time to take their table, and as Kathryn seated herself opposite Steve, she attempted to regain her carefree mood. After all, if she couldn't relax with her cousin and old friends, whom could she relax with?

At least the menu looked promising, with an emphasis on provincial French cooking and seasonal ingredients. She opted for onion soup with crusty bread as a starter, with Cassoulet and a fresh green salad to follow, then turned to the wine list with interest. May as well choose the finest on the menu, she decided, as she offered her opinions on what to drink with the first course. Determined to make this an evening to remember, she replaced the menu on the table and joined in the general conversation.

The wine when it came proved a winner, with a distinctive flavor that left a delicious tang at the back of the throat. David was in good form, and as she laughed at his jokes, she felt her tension begin to drift away. Her thoughts returned briefly to Gerard, and she wondered whether he had come to drink or dine, whether he was on his own or with someone.

Partway through their main course he entered the restaurant with Sarah Vine. Heads turned as the tall, distinguished-looking man escorted the sleek blonde toward a candlelit table set at a discreet distance from the rest of the diners.

Sarah was wearing a mini-dress in a shimmering blue material; it left little to the imagination. To think Kathryn had begun to wonder if her rejection of Gerard had been unnecessarily harsh! He had no need of her sympathy, with the delectable Sarah hanging on to his every word. She observed them with a sidelong glance as they seated themselves, and although a large hothouse palm obscured her view of Gerard, she had a feeling he could see her.

She gave a shrill laugh, leaned forward to clasp Steve's hands, and gave him what she hoped was a charming smile. It was some time since she'd practiced flirtation techniques and she hoped she wasn't hopelessly rusty. At least Steve seemed to appreciate her, the way he was leaning across the table, lips pursed. She kissed him lightly on his waiting lips, then resisted the impulse to wipe her mouth with her napkin.

The food was cooked to perfection, and the wine was slipping down with ease. As a rule Kathryn drank very little but this light-headed feeling was a delicious novelty and she made no attempt at self-control. By the time the coffee came she had lost the thread of the conversation, and was surprised when David and Jenny stood up and announced their departure.

"You're going?" she asked, surprised.

"We've just said so, love," said David patiently. "Jenny's got a headache and I'm taking her home."

Jenny was looking rather pale, come to think of it. After patting her hand sympathetically, she turned back to her cousin. "How will you get home?" she asked vaguely.

"Cab's on its way," he replied. "It should be here any minute." He leaned over to give her a farewell peck on the cheek. "And that's how you'll have to get back," he whispered, jerking his head in Steve's direction.

Glancing across the table Kathryn took his point. Steve was downing yet another glass of wine. "Don't worry," she hissed back, "I'll organize transportation. Off you go, and take care of Jenny."

They left and Kathryn ordered more coffee, hoping the strong, dark brew would have a sobering effect.

Now that they were alone, Steve's mood changed. Clasping Kathryn's hands, he began a long maudlin discourse on his relationship with Susannah, his ex-girlfriend. Kathryn made sympathetic noises, genuinely sorry for him, but the sound of his voice was beginning to grate on her swimming senses, and he was holding her hands far too tightly.

Live music drifted in from the bar and Steve, with a manic change of mood, stood up, pulling Kathryn with him, declaring he wanted to dance all night. With her hand shackled to his side, Kathryn decided it was easier to comply. She followed him next door to the dance floor, where he pulled her into his arms before beginning an unsteady progress around the floor.

Over Steve's shoulder she noticed a small crowd drifting in from the restaurant. Head and shoulders above them walked Gerard, Sarah by his side, matching him for style and glamour. She moved into his arms, their movements synchronizing with the easy rhythm of the dance music. He had not looked in her direction, not once.

Kathryn leaned back and smiled invitingly into Steve's face, her arms encircling his neck. Steve's mouth swooped. She expressed delight as they continued to circle the dance floor. The music changed gear, speeding into a faster, pulsating tempo, as Kathryn pulled apart from her partner, her natural sense of rhythm evident in every movement. As she looked across at Steve, he was moving unsteadily from one foot to the other, fixing her with an admiring glance. She basked in his approval, heady on adrenaline, as her swirling senses attempted to keep up with the rapid beat. The music reached a crescendo as she swung around in a dramatic finale, only to find herself in the arms of Gerard Fitzalan.

"If you want to spare yourself further embarrassment, I suggest you look as though you're enjoying this." He linked his hands behind her back, pinning her arms to her side as he began to move her in time to the music, which had now slowed to a gentler rhythm.

"But, I'm not enjoying this," Kathryn insisted fiercely, "and I'm not supposed to be with you. You're not Steve."

"No, I'm not—thankfully." He swung her around, pointing her in the direction of where Steve now sat at a side table, head in hands, looking ghostly white.

"Is that what you want, Kathryn?" he asked, his voice grating. "A callow youth who turns the evening into a waste?"

"That's unfair," Kathryn protested. "Poor Steve . . ."

"Poor Steve is about to collapse any moment, leaving you stranded."

"No problem," said Kathryn. "When we're ready to leave I'll order a taxi."

Gerard's tone was skeptical. "Try getting a cab to come to an out of the way place like this after midnight. You'll have a long wait." He gripped Kathryn's chin, forcing her head upward to meet his unyielding stare. "Get your things, Kathryn. I'm taking you and your friend home."

Kathryn's jaw tightened. How dare he look at her as though she were beneath contempt. He had no right to wade in with unwanted advice. Besides, he had his own date, that blonde bimbo to attend to— why should he want to interfere with her social life?

"Well?"

"Thanks—but no thanks." She managed to hold his gaze. "Steve and I prefer to make our own way home." She freed herself from his arms with a downward thrust of both elbows. She walked across to Steve with as much dignity as she could muster. When she reached Steve's table she collapsed on a stool because she suddenly felt tired.

Steve, sensing her distress, patted her hand sympathetically. "Never mind, Kath, soon get you home." He fished in his pockets, his movements uncoordinated. "Just find the keys."

"No!" Kathryn pulled his hands away from his pockets. "I'll go and order a taxi. Just stay here, Steve. Please!"

The staff at the reception desk was helpful but one or two calls to local taxi firms proved fruitless. They promised to keep trying, and Kathryn turned away, dispirited. If need be, Steve and I will walk home, she determined, reentering the bar. Steve was nowhere to be seen. With an awful presentiment she dashed back into the reception area and ran up to the swinging doors leading to the outside. Through the glass she could see Steve's shambling figure moving across the parking lot, no doubt heading for his vehicle.

Without waiting for her coat she shot through the doors, cursing under her breath as the cold air laden with water droplets cut through to the bone. She raced along and managed to catch up with Steve as he reached his car and fell awkwardly against the hood.

"Ah, Kathryn," he mumbled, as she came to a shuddering halt. "Where've you been? Time to go now." He lurched forward and began a clumsy attempt to fit his key into the lock of the driver's door.

"Steve! You're not fit to drive." Kathryn's breathing was labored as her hands reached forward. "Give those keys to me—please!"

Giggling, Steve held the keys out of reach as Kathryn tried to capture them. Tussling with him, her fingers closed over the keys as the threatened downpour became reality, and they were both drenched with ice-cold, sleeting rain. Steve crumpled, and as Kathryn attempted to pull him away, he pushed her roughly from him.

He was quite beyond reason, and she knew she'd

have to ask the restaurant staff for help. At least she had his car keys; he couldn't drive off. She began to retrace her footsteps through the dimly lit parking lot, hurrying in an attempt to reach the refuge of the restaurant.

She never saw the pothole. She only knew of its existence after she tripped onto her hands and knees into the muddied hole. She scrambled up, looking with dismay at her filthy hands and torn stockings. She was soaked through, her hair was plastered to her head like a skullcap, and now she looked as though she'd been mugged. How much worse could this evening get?

"Kathryn?"

Now she knew. She raised her arm to protect her eyes from the glare of a powerful flashlight, and the light was immediately dimmed.

"What on earth happened . . . ?" Gerard's voice trailed away as the sound of groans drew his attention to where Steve was slumped against his car. "I see. Well, you'd better let me take you home now. Get in the car." He flicked the flashlight toward a dark Mercedes, the light picking out a neat blonde head resting nonchalantly against the headrest of the passenger seat, sapphire blue eyes turned toward them.

"I will not," Kathryn spat out. She could see he was taken aback by her venom, but the frustrations of this disastrous evening had taken a toll on her temper. She drew herself up, ice edging her words. "I'm going inside now. The staff will help me with Steve and we'll organize some way to get home."

"You can't go inside looking like that!"

She shrugged, raising muddied hands. "So, I've had a little accident. They'll understand."

"You look positively indecent—look at yourself."

Kathryn looked down. The rain had eased off now, but the damage was done. Her dress clung to her like soggy tissue paper, outlining every curve, while the neckline had sagged as much as the hemline had shrunk. She really would strangle that saleswoman!

"I'm not letting you go into a public place looking as though you're in a wet T-shirt competition," he hissed.

"It's none of your business," Kathryn sparked back, "and it comes ripe from a man whose date for the evening wears little short of . . . of . . . beachwear!"

"Kathryn—my patience is just about at an end. Get into the car—please!"

Kathryn's chin rose even higher. "I'll crawl home before I accept a lift with you, and there's nothing you can do about it!"

"Oh, no?"

She should not have issued such a reckless challenge and realized her mistake a moment later, when he ducked, wrapped his arms around her legs, and upended her over his shoulder as though she were feather-light.

Her stomach lurched, and she closed her eyes to avoid the disorienting view of an upside down world as she was carried toward the car and then bundled, protesting, into the rear of the Mercedes. As she hit the luxurious pale blue upholstery the fight went out of her, and she collapsed into a corner as another wave of dizziness disordered her senses. She remembered the light coming on briefly then Steve joined her, falling heavily against her, his head lolling against her shoulder.

She remembered little of the journey back but realized they had entered the stableyard when the car swung sharply to the right. The vehicle came to a halt, and Kathryn began to sit up, her arms going around Steve protectively, as she attempted to wake him and push him upright. He'd have to spend the night at her place, of course. She'd bed him down on the couch and sort out his hangover in the morning.

She blinked as the light lit up the dim interior. Steve had an inane grin on his face and was starting to come round, but she still had her arms around him, fearful lest he should collapse. Without warning the door opened and Gerard's arm snaked between them, pushing Steve away from her with one brusque movement.

"We'll take the gentleman home. No doubt his address is in his wallet."

Kathryn started to protest but her words didn't seem to be making much sense. She still had Steve's car keys in her hand—she must at least give him those—but when she reached toward him, she found her wrist gripped by Gerard's free hand as he turned to her with, "Get out of the car, Kathryn. We'll make sure he's all right."

She scrambled out of the vehicle to stand forlornly in the headlights as Gerard backed up, aware that at least one pair of eyes was watching her. Sarah was staring over the dashboard at her, blue eyes blazing triumphantly.

Chapter Five

The next morning Kathryn told David the whole story. "I made a complete fool of myself," she concluded.

"I think you're being too tough on yourself. Most people go a little crazy now and again. It's a way of letting off steam."

"Not for me," she protested.

"Maybe that's the problem. You work very hard and don't socialize much. Perhaps you need a better balance in your life?"

Kathryn digested his words in silence. Summed up in his blunt, big brotherly way, her life did sound desperately dull, and the thought rattled her.

Kathryn felt washed out for the rest of the day and, forewarned by David, neither Jean or Harry inquired about her evening out. And that's how I want it, she mused, the whole event consigned to oblivion. As for Gerard, she could not bear the thought of seeing him at all. He had witnessed one of the most humiliating evenings of her life and must have have found the contrast between her and the New York sophisticates he was used to squiring painfully clear. She determined to avoid him and this proved remarkably easy, as he no longer appeared at the stables each day to exercise Sebastian.

After a week Kathryn's curiosity got the better of her, and she inquired after him when she and David were cleaning tack.

David was vague. "Not sure, really. Some flunky rang from the Manor, said not to expect him." He glanced over at her. "I don't suppose you've had a chance to thank him yet—for bringing you home."

Kathryn made a noncommittal remark and bent over her task, her hair falling forward, hiding the color in her cheeks.

"I'm not surprised he went out of his way to help you," David continued. "He's terribly attracted to you."

Kathryn's head shot up. "Don't be silly."

"Oh, I'm right. He was looking daggers at our table when we were in the restaurant."

"He did seem to have a problem with Steve," Kathryn conceded.

"Oh, he wasn't looking daggers at Steve," David said blithely. "It was at you."

* * *

Confirmation of Gerard's whereabouts came during a prickly encounter with Sarah in the village general store. Kathryn entered to find Sarah trawling through the packets of tights on the shelves, making highly audible sounds of dissatisfaction. She looked charming clad in a well-tailored pants suit in cream jersey. It enhanced her small, curvaceous figure and showed off her tan, chunky gold jewelry, and with a scarlet scarf thrown casually around her neck adding a splash of color.

How dare she be so elegant just for a trip to the village shop, Kathryn thought, painfully aware of her warm but shabby jacket and old cord trousers.

Sarah turned at Kathryn's approach. "Really," she said, raising her slim shoulders. "Have they never heard of Lycra in this place?"

Embarrassed, Kathryn looked over to where Mrs. Tipton was serving a customer. "We only have a small village shop," she explained stiffly. "It's quite well stocked, considering."

"I'll take your word for it—as a local," Sarah said, emphasizing the last word as if she were describing a contagious disease.

"You must be longing for a speedy return to Manhattan," Kathryn said, determined not to let her annoyance show.

"Absolutely," Sarah drawled. "Of course, Gerard's there already. His interest in this part of the world seems to have died down, thank goodness.

Hardly surprising when one considers . . ." Her eyes swept meaningfully over Kathryn and then she turned sharply, thrusting the packets of tights back on the shelves. "Better get back. Gerard's phoning with details of my one-way ticket out of here. Ciao!" She swept out of the shop, a seraphic smile crossing her neat, doll-like features.

Kathryn seethed inwardly, then reminded herself that she had found out what she needed to know. Gerard had returned to the States, probably on a permanent basis. No need to skulk around for fear of bumping into him—she would be able to reclaim her peace of mind, return to the tranquil life she valued so much. Waiting for relief to wash over her, she was disturbed when all she experienced was a dull sense of anticlimax, a feeling that something intrinsically exciting had been stolen from her.

Over the next few days this empty feeling persisted, and she came to the reluctant conclusion that Gerard's intrusion in her life had highlighted the emotional void at the heart of it. He, of course, was quite unsuitable to fill it. But someone else? Steve, perhaps?

If enthusiasm was the criterion then Steve would fit the bill. He had inundated her with flowers and apologetic notes after their disastrous evening together, but so far she had refused to meet him. Now that painful memories were fading, however, she realized how unfair she was being. Steve had been let down badly and had set out to drown his sorrows, while she had behaved just as foolishly without any excuse!

She arranged to meet him in the village pub and was amused when she arrived to find him nursing a large mineral water.

"Kathryn!" He rose, kissing her nervously on the cheek. "Let me get you something to drink."

"In a moment." Kathryn patted the seat beside her. "I think we need to clear the air first."

"Sure." Steve sat down, his jumpiness seeming to increase as he turned toward her.

Kathryn drew a deep breath. "I'll be blunt, Steve. Our first date was a disaster, but I was to blame just as much as you. We both behaved like a pair of clowns. I think we need to forget the whole episode—and start over. If you'd like to, that is?" she added shyly.

"Like to?" He leaned forward and clasped her hand as his eyes sparkled their reply and the tension between them dissolved.

Kathryn watched Steve as he went to the bar, feeling pleasantly complacent. Steve was good company; they laughed at the same things, and shared similar backgrounds and interests. Surely they would prove compatible? He was, after all, from her world.

More dates followed and, as is the way with small communities, they were soon perceived as an "item." Kathryn enjoyed their outings and knew that in many ways Steve was the ideal date for her. He was affectionate and caring but willing to comply with the boundaries she set. They were not yet ready to deepen their relationship, for Steve was still getting over Susannah, and she . . . ? Well, she was just not ready.

Douglas Talbot was in full charge of the Manor, and renovations proceeded at a rapid rate. Kathryn persuaded Ken Morris to establish links with Talbot and report back to the Parish Council on the changes taking shape.

Ken had nothing but praise for the refurbishment of the house, reassured by the fact that the whole enterprise was being masterminded by a distinguished architect who specialized in restoring period properties. Kathryn's fears of wholesale destruction appeared unfounded, as only a small proportion of the house would be used as a conventional office, leaving the bulk of the property to be used as a deluxe hospitality suite to woo potential customers and entertain business associates. The Manor gardens were to be landscaped and the grounds managed professionally to assist the diverse wildlife in the area.

It all sounded marvelous, Kathryn thought, listening to Ken's latest report one dank November evening—yet a nagging doubt remained. If the new owners were so efficient and well meaning, why was Uncle Harry still waiting for the written agreement that would ensure their future? Harry had been told that he would be dealt with as soon as the attorneys had sorted out Lady Alice's chaotic affairs. Kathryn had greeted this news skeptically, but the rest of the family seemed content to carry on as normal and bide their time, convinced that Gerard had not lied to them, that their position was secure.

Unwilling to cause her uncle distress, Kathryn stayed silent but resolved to keep a close eye on what was happening locally. She appeared to be the only one with doubts, as most villagers welcomed the changes wrought by the new owners, especially when jobs were advertised which would suit school graduates who were currently facing unemployment or migration to larger towns.

Of Gerard, Kathryn heard very little. He appeared to be concentrating on their Stateside operation to the exclusion of the company's new acquisition in England. So be it, she told herself, on more than one occasion. Life was so full at the moment she had no time to squander thoughts on a spoiled business tycoon who had waltzed into her life and then waltzed out of it without a second thought.

Work was claiming its full share of her attention. As Christmas approached, she received an invitation to hold an exhibition in early spring at a small but prestigious art gallery in Buxton, their county town.

She accepted immediately; it would mean a lot of hard work but she knew that, handled right, it could be a turning point in her career.

In the meantime she had Christmas to look forward to. Jean and Harry came from old, local families, and traditionally, Hollinswood Stables was the center of hospitality over the festive season. Assorted friends and relatives swelled their numbers to sixteen sitting down to Christmas lunch, and as always, Jean organized her kitchen with military precision to produce a spectacular traditional meal, the table groaning beneath a massive turkey and attendant trimmings.

Steve had been invited for Christmas Day, and Kathryn knew they were a focus for speculation. Relatives and friends asked pointed questions and nodded their heads in knowing fashion.

So what. She and Steve knew the score, and no amount of gossip or innuendo would transform it into what it wasn't—yet. She did have a nasty moment though, after lunch, when Steve handed her present over. Christmas packaging could not disguise the shape of a small, square jeweler's box. Nervously she tore the paper off and hoped her relief was not too obvious when she opened the case to reveal an exquisite jet brooch.

"It's perfect," she breathed, tracing the stones set in a delicate circular pattern with her fingertips. "Where on earth did you find it?"

"Trawled the antique shops in Whitby." He grinned ruefully. "And I've got the blisters on my feet to prove it. But I know how fond you are of jet. When I saw that piece I knew it was just right for you."

Dear Steve, he was so thoughtful. She kissed him on the lips then helped him fasten the brooch on to the lapel of her soft, coffee-colored wool dress. She watched anxiously as he unwrapped her present from him and was relieved when his features lit up with delight.

"That's the view from Wynatt's Hill," she told him, peering over his shoulder at the framed landscape.

"I know where it is." He smiled sideways at her. "And it's my favorite view." His mouth sought hers, much to the relish of various family members who were following the encounter by the fireplace with interest.

Christmas had brought them closer, much closer, and as the New Year approached Kathryn began to wonder whether it was time to move the relationship on. She was deeply fond of him, and, importantly, she knew she could trust him. Surely that was enough?

The New Year beckoned enticingly. Everyone in the village had received invitations to a ball at the Manor to see in the New Year and celebrate the completion of the first phase of renovation. It was a wonderful opportunity to see the interior of the house again and a good excuse for a glamorous night out.

Kathryn and Jean went in search of new outfits, trying on different garments in a variety of shops and giggling like schoolgirls at the more outlandish creations. Eventually Jean opted for a full-length gown in black velvet with a V-neckline and a matching quilted jacket with pearl buttons.

"You look superb," Kathryn told her aunt, who primped in front of the large, ornate mirror.

"I do, don't I?" she agreed, admiring her reflection. She began to take off the garment reluctantly. "What we need now is to find something equally terrific for you."

That proved easier said than done. Several hours later, footsore and with the best of the day over, Kathryn was on the verge of giving up when, on impulse, she walked into a small boutique that specialized in selling clothes from the developing world. Jean persuaded her to try on a two-piece outfit in a filmy brown Indian cotton shot through with golden thread. The full-length skirt fell in soft folds from the tight waistband, while the short-sleeved top, similar to those worn under saris, ended just above it allowing a tiny sliver of midriff to show.

Kathryn was unsure. "It's a little unconventional for such a formal occasion."

Jean had no doubts. "So what? That gorgeous

fabric suits your coloring and the style shows off your figure. Go for it, girl."

Kathryn twirled in a sudden high-spirited gesture, the full skirt billowing out around her, the decision made.

On New Year's Eve Kathryn sat at her dressing table and watched with trepidation as Jean created a new hairstyle for her. Until now she had resisted Jean's attempts to restyle her hair, even though her aunt had trained as a hairdresser before her marriage.

"You're just not adventurous enough, Kath, that's your trouble." Jean took a brush to Kathryn's hair, ignoring Kathryn's agonized look. "You have a lovely face, a long neck, and fine bone structure. If we take your hair away from your face we can highlight your best features."

Kathryn eyed herself in the mirror. Jean had gathered her hair into a ponytail high on her head. Now she took the thick ponytail, brushed it into a fan shape, and wove fine gilt thread decorated with tiny golden beads into the coppery strands.

She stood back, satisfied. "There—all done. Quick, easy, effective."

Delighted, Kathryn moved her head as the ponytail flicked from side to side, shimmering in the pale lamplight. "Well, I would never have thought . . ." She caught sight of Jean's expression and leaped up to give her a hug. "Thank you, Aunt Jean . . . it's brilliant." She ushered her out of the room. "Now you go and pamper yourself," she ordered. "I'll see you downstairs later."

Douglas Talbot was at the door to greet their party, his welcome warm and assured as he ushered them into the large entrance hall crammed with an assortment of well-dressed guests. It was so crowded it was difficult to see what changes had been made, but the oak paneling glowed warmly, the carvings on the mantel of the newly cleaned stone fireplace could now be seen in detail, and all damp spots seemed to have been eradicated from the ornate plasterwork ceiling. Kathryn stood looking upward, enjoying the sight of the now pristine Jacobean ceiling. Preoccupied, she did not notice the man descending the curved staircase until she overheard a remark that caused her to glance in his direction. Gerard Fitzalan had reached the bottom step and now stood surveying the throng. Kathryn's heart seemed to tilt forward in her chest, and she pulled her wrap from her shoulders, her whole body suffused with unexpected warmth.

He was in formal dress, the black suit, white pleated silk shirt, and bow tie emphasizing the controlled strength of his tall, rangy figure. His hair seemed longer and boyishly unruly as it escaped its sleek styling to fall across his forehead and brush his collar in rakish fashion. He towered above the crowd in more ways than one, and Kathryn found it impossible to tear her eyes away from him.

Cool gray eyes beneath arched brows scrutinized the assembled company, then stopped and rested on Kathryn herself. Every muscle in her body seemed to tense as he moved toward her, guests moving aside automatically as his charismatic figure swept by.

Pleasure colored his features as, hand outstretched, he reached toward her. She shrank back, fearful even of the lightest touch of his fingers.

"Harry! How good to see you. How are you?" Gerard's hand reached beyond her to draw her uncle to his side as Kathryn stepped back abruptly.

A broad, middle-aged man moved in front of her, blocking her view of Gerard and crushing her foot in the bargain. The pain was almost a relief, something to focus her disordered senses on as she fought for control. Calm down, she told herself frantically, as her heart continued to pound. Surely it had been the shock of the unexpected which had caused her to react in such a potent way to Gerard's presence. She was on the verge of a serious relationship with another man, so there could be no other explanation. Besides, she reminded herself, he was completely indifferent to her existence. He hadn't even noticed her.

The throng in front of her moved on, and she saw

Steve gesturing to her from the doorway of the Great Hall. She moved forward eagerly and reached his side, drawing his arm through hers.

"Let's get out of this scrum," he suggested. "Refreshments this way, I believe."

They passed through into the Great Hall, where food and drink was being served from long tables clothed in crisp, white linen and decorated with centerpieces of ferns and hothouse exotics, which expelled a heady perfume into the air. Wall lamps, held by elegant silver sconces, filtered light through mottled green and blue glass shades to lend a soft glow to the large rectangular room. The heavy, wood-paneled walls were garlanded with wreaths of fresh greenery intertwined with tiny silver bells, and the huge central chandelier had been repaired and refurbished, its tall white candlesticks aflame as the whole piece glistened like one enormous splintered diamond.

"This place has been transformed!" Kathryn drank in the magical scene, turning aside only to take the tall stemmed glass filled to the brim by Steve. The guests now began to stream into the hall. "Most of the village seems to be here," she remarked, nodding to the postmistress, who was a vision in ruby red velvet.

"And many more besides. There's quite a few people here I don't recognize. Company folk, I guess." Kathryn murmured agreement, slightly amused at how conspicuous the strangers were with their deep suntans and well-groomed, expensive appearances.

The musicians, seated appropriately in the minstrel's gallery at the far end of the room, struck up a Strauss waltz, and a handsome, elderly couple began to glide across the highly polished floor. Others followed suit, and Kathryn watched in delight as, officially, the ball began.

As she drank in the atmosphere, she began to relax, thankful that her pulse, at least, had returned to normal. What a fool she had been to react to Gerard like that—but she had been totally unprepared for his sudden appearance! She supposed he was still greeting guests at the door; he was nowhere to be seen in the now crowded ballroom.

Jenny and David whirled past, flashing happy grins, and Steve was galvanized into action, his arm encircling Kathryn as they moved onto the dance floor. Kathryn's waltzing skills were negligible, but she did her best to follow Steve's lead, surprised at how well she performed as she moved in time to the music. One dance followed another as the musicians alternated sets of traditional dance music with contemporary upbeat rhythms.

At last they stopped for a breather, joining Harry and Jean at the buffet bar, where the selection of delicacies was mouth-watering, served with great aplomb by staff in dark green uniforms.

"They've done us proud," Harry remarked, mouth half filled with salmon terrine. "Not a paper plate in sight." He nodded toward the crockery, which was, diplomatically, classic English chinaware from a local pottery.

But where was the owner of all this opulence? Douglas Talbot was ensconced in the far corner, talking to a short, balding man in a dark suit, but his boss was nowhere to be seen. Kathryn sent Steve off to dance with Jean while she sat out with her uncle, eyes once more scanning the dance floor. To her surprise, David and Sarah Vine swung into view, bright blond heads close as they swayed in time to the rhythms. What on earth were they doing together? Jenny would hardly mind—she knew David was a free spirit—but what would Gerard think? Wasn't New Year's Eve a special time when couples wished to be together?

Steve returned, his energy hardly depleted, and when he enticed Kathryn on to the dance floor once more, she gave herself up to the music, thoroughly enjoying the atmosphere and Steve's easy company.

As Kathryn applauded the musicians at the end of a set, she realized with a start how late it was. Her feet were aching, and she was hot and sticky. At this rate she'd be completely exhausted by the time they reached midnight. She told Steve she was going to the powder room and, finding it congested, was directed by a member of staff to an overspill room on the first floor, in the west wing.

Kathryn pushed open the door of the powder room and stood for a moment, transfixed by the transformation of what had once been a rather dusty lumber room. Mirrored walls made the room seem much larger, and the brassware and gleaming ceramics were practical and chic without the brashness of some modern conversions. She crossed to the mirror, her heels digging into the royal blue deep pile carpet patterned with tiny, golden fleur de lys. The place was empty and she took her time, bathing her hands and face, then redoing her light makeup. After adding a dash of subtle French perfume to her wrists, she began to retrace her footsteps.

She paused at the head of the stairs, her hand resting lightly on the carved oak newel post as she looked down on the heads of the revelers below. On impulse, she stepped back into the shadows, her head turning toward the dimly lit corridors of the east wing. Those rooms had been turned into private apartments—that much Kathryn had gleaned from Ken's reports—and one of them had been Lady Alice's bedroom. She would dearly love to see what they had done to it. One peek, then out.

She sped lightly along the corridor, holding up her full skirt with one hand. One, two, three. Yes, this was the one. The door, minus its old creak, opened smoothly, and what Kathryn saw drew her right into the bedroom.

It was so different! Kathryn had spent many hours in this room, nursing Lady Alice in her last illness. All traces of the ramshackle chaos of an old lady's final resting place had been removed, and now new crimson damask curtains clothed the latticed windows. The same material had been used to renew the hangings on the fourposter bed. An antique Oriental rug of grays and reds partially covered the delightfully uneven floorboards, and the stark white walls were dotted with Victorian hunting scenes and rural landscapes in dark frames. The linen press and chest of drawers in blackened oak, carved into complex patterns by long-dead Jacobean craftsmen, had been cleared of Lady Alice's clutter and could now be seen in all their glory. Having taken in the changes wrought in the room, Kathryn's eyes now fell on the fine gold Rolex watch lying casually on the bed. She recognized that watch.

The door handle rattled and Kathryn darted forward through the half-open door in front of her. She reached her refuge just in time as, trembling, she stood and listened to movements in the master bedroom. The bathroom she was now hiding in must have been created out of the old dressing room. With its chrome taps, dark gray marbled basin, and black and white tiles in geometric patterns, it was uncompromising in its masculinity. Kathryn breathed in the distinctive scent of aftershave lotion while its owner moved around a few feet from her, oblivious to her presence.

It was only a few moments, though it felt like hours. Then a door closed, leaving complete silence.

Thank goodness! Kathryn touched her forehead, brushing away perspiration as the hammering in her chest began to subside. Better make a move, quickly.

She crept out of the bedroom and began to cross the room, eyes fixed firmly on the door handle ahead, when a whirring sound drew her attention to the left-hand side of the bed. Too late she remembered the sliding panel that gave access to the room next door. Her feet rooted to the spot as the gap in the panel widened and Gerard Fitzalan stepped into the room.

Chapter Six

Shocked brown eyes meshed with gray as time seemed to hang on a second and, involuntarily, she found herself taking in every aspect of his appearance. He was without a jacket or tie, his long hair disheveled and his pleated shirt wide open at the neck, the dark body hair contrasting starkly with the whiteness of the shirt.

Mentally she shook herself, dragging her eyes from his to focus on the door handle, her body poised for flight.

"Not so fast!" For such a tall man he moved swiftly, cutting across her path to reach the door before she could move one step forward. Her hands curled into tight balls of frustration as her exit was blocked, and Gerard showed every sign of enjoying her discomfort, lounging against the door as though he had all the time in the world.

His lips curved into an insolent smile. "Kathryn! You make a habit of blundering into my private space, don't you?"

Kathryn took one step back. "Yes . . . well, I'm sorry. I was just . . ."

His brows rose. "Looking? I've heard that somewhere before." She steeled herself to stand still as he advanced toward her, menace implicit in every line of his tall, muscular body. He stood, eyes slanting down at her, silver irises aflame with a soft mocking light. "If you'd wanted a visit, you should have spoken to me privately. We could have arranged something."

Heat raced through her veins. She knew he was deliberately provoking her, but his words belittled the attraction she was desperately fighting against. She needed to hit back and chose the first words that came to mind. "I have no interest in you, Gerard, as I've made clear from the beginning!"

To her consternation, he threw his head back and began to laugh, a deep-throated chuckle that served only to fuel her anger. She went to brush past him only to find one arm seized as she was pulled toward him. "So—you have no interest in me at all? I think the lady doth protest too much."

"And you presume too much!" She attempted to pull her arm away but found it held fast. She lowered her lashes to escape his compelling gaze, his nearness causing her heart to beat at an alarming rate.

He homed in on her discomfort. "If you're so indifferent to me, Kathryn, why are you trembling so much?"

"Anger." Kathryn spoke through stiffened lips. Although determined not to give in to his blandishments she was afraid her resolve would weaken if he did not release her very soon. "I think you'd better let me go," she warned. "Steve will wonder where I am."

Her strategy worked better than she dared hope. His hand fell from her arm and he stepped to one side. "If your boyfriend awaits you, Kathryn, then you'd better go."

For one moment his words startled her. Surely he didn't think she and Steve were seriously involved? Perhaps it was better that he believed her to be committed to another man, she reasoned, as she hurried past him to reach the door, grasping the brass doorknob with moistened palms. She threw one backward glance into the room, intending to leave with a triumphant flourish. What she saw caused her to hesitate, her heart seeming to stop as she took in Gerard's motionless figure. He seemed to be in a lonely world of his own, shoulders bunched and head lowered, as though nursing some secret pain. Struck by his vulnerability, by the first chink she had ever detected in Gerard's armor of self-possession, she acted purely from instinct. Returning to him, fingers interlinking with his, she pulled him toward her, and as his head lowered, it seemed only natural to reach up to kiss him gently on the lips. Meant as a gesture of comfort, it was a lingering, tender kiss. Gerard groaned, his lips becoming more demanding as he drew her closer, and Kathryn found herself responding in kind, twining her arms around his neck, her fingers lacing through the silky strands of his hair as she found herself matching his growing ardor.

As though from a far distant country, Kathryn's punch-drunk senses recorded the sound of clock chimes. The significance of the twelve notes bit into her like the thrust of cold steel. Midnight—New Year's! Steve would wonder what on earth had happened to her. He'd come looking for her, and they'd be discovered. This was madness! She tensed and Gerard noticed immediately. His lips left hers to say, "Kate, what is it?"

Her voice was barely audible. "It's midnight—New Year's! They'll wonder where I am—come looking for me."

"So," he growled, "we'll lock the door. But we can't stop now, Kate."

It was no good. Reality had penetrated her sensual dream, and she knew she couldn't humiliate Steve by staying with Gerard while he waited for her downstairs. He deserved better. She must break with him first, then try to sort out her tangled feelings for Gerard. That would be fair to all concerned.

She disentangled herself, hardly daring to look up into his face. "I came with Steve and I have to go back downstairs and see the New Year in with him." She struggled to find the words to describe her feelings. "You see, he's been badly hurt once and I don't want—"

"You should have thought of that earlier—before you fell into my arms!"

Gerard's features were tight with fury. She couldn't blame him for being angry. She was handling everything so badly, and before she could gather her thoughts, she was subjected to another accusation. "Is this how you get your kicks, Kathryn, by leading men on, then dropping them as soon as they respond?"

Kathryn flinched, exhaling one word, "No!"

"Really? I'm not so sure." He turned away before she could defend herself further, his voice becoming distant as he crossed the room. "Go back to your boyfriend, Kathryn. You're out of your league here." The door slammed shut on his bitter words, the noise echoing around the room like the rhythm that was beginning to beat a tattoo within Kathryn's temple.

She felt cold and hot at the same time and had little memory of her return to the party through groups of New Year's revelers, but the look on

Steve's face as she hurried toward him revealed what sort of a sight she must look. She stammered her apologies, made excuses about a headache, and was very relieved when Jean declared that she would drive her straight home, as she looked "dreadful."

Steve insisted on coming with them, and when they reached the flat she was glad of his presence. He made her a milky drink, helped her into the bedroom, and deposited a chaste kiss on her cheek before tiptoeing from the room.

As Kathryn drifted into sleep she reflected on the irony of the situation. Steve had been kindness itself, but now she knew there never could be anything serious between them. No substitute would do for Gerard Fitzalan, the man who had stolen her heart, the man who had just left her with contempt in his eyes.

In the morning she felt little better. Her head was still throbbing, and she felt feverish, the slightest activity sapping her strength. By the evening she was back in bed with a raging temperature. A concerned Jean brought in the doctor, who informed her in an overly cheerful manner that she had succumbed to influenza and a few days in bed would soon see her fit.

The doctor's prognosis proved optimistic. It was ten days before Kathryn began to feel well again and a further week before she regained her strength.

During her convalescence she had much time to brood on the rift between herself and Gerard. Their brief encounter had served only to reveal the true state of her feelings for him. She berated herself for not explaining herself clearly when she had the chance, and she knew she could not allow Gerard to go on believing that she had set out to tease and humiliate him as a mere diversion. Apprehension welled up inside her, but she knew she had to see Gerard and explain herself, swallow her pride, and tell him the true state of affairs between herself and Steve. Otherwise there would be no chance of breaching the chasm between them.

A cool January morning found Kathryn walking up the Manor driveway, heart beating in time to her brisk footsteps as she contemplated the daunting prospect before her. She had decided on the direct approach, since all attempts to arrange a meeting by phone had foundered. Distant receptionist voices had insisted that Mr. Fitzalan was "not available," so she had decided to find out in person what that meant.

She turned the bend in the driveway which brought the Manor into view and stopped to drink in a scene which had changed considerably since she had last seen the house in daylight. A gleaming, corporate headquarters was rising, phoenix-like, out of the careworn, rather shabby, building Kathryn had grown up with. Renovations highlighted architectural features once lost to damp and decay, and the whole building looked as though it had been scoured and reassembled, losing none of its charm in the process.

A parking bay to the right of the front door was filled with a selection of upmarket models, and moving closer, she could see the corporate logo displayed proudly above each registration number. It was all very impressive—and very intimidating! What right had she to fall in love with the owner of all this wealth? She wanted to turn and run but, stiffening her inner resolve, she walked up to the front door and slammed the ringed iron knocker against the studded door with some semblance of calm.

The door swung back and a man with iron-gray hair, wearing a dark suit and the studied indifference of a professional butler, peered out at her.

"I would like to speak to Mr. Fitzalan," Kathryn said. "My name is Kathryn Beaumont."

One eyebrow arched delicately. "Mr. Fitzalan is absent. If you care to leave a message . . ."

"Can I help, Miss Beaumont?" The butler disappeared from view to be replaced by the tall figure of Douglas Talbot. "Come in, please."

Rather reluctantly, Kathryn stepped into the gloom of the hall and was then ushered by Douglas Talbot into a room on the left. It was now an office cunningly disguised as a gentleman's study, with classic oak fitted furniture and floor to ceiling shelving filled with beautifully bound books. Douglas drew up a winged leather armchair for Kathryn to seat herself, then leaned nonchalantly against his desk, his tanned features crinkling into a friendly smile. "Well, Miss Beaumont, what may I do for you?"

Kathryn's mouth felt dry and she swallowed nervously. "I wonder if it's possible to see Mr. Fitzalan. I need to speak to him on a ... personal matter."

Blue incisive eyes swept Kathryn's face. "He's not here, I'm afraid. He's in the States troubleshooting on a major project we're involved with."

"In that case," Kathryn said, her hands twisting in her lap, "perhaps I could have his phone number in New York." She felt almost relieved at his absence. It might be easier speaking her mind if the Atlantic was between them.

"You could, except that he's not in New York. He's in Alaska and notorious for going off into the wilds without a mobile phone."

"I see." She rose, dispirited. "Thank you for your time, Mr. Talbot." He, at least, had treated her with some courtesy. "I'll see myself out, please don't trouble yourself." She was almost at the door when he called her back.

"Miss Beaumont, wait a moment. I should be able to get a message through to Gerard. What say I ask him to contact you at the stables. Would that be satisfactory?"

Kathryn agreed eagerly. "Oh, yes—it would be!"

"Good." His eyes lightened as he flashed her a knowing smile. "Don't worry about a thing, I'll make sure Gerard gets your message."

Kathryn left, feeling pleased that she had made some attempt to heal the breech between her and Gerard. Now it was merely a matter of waiting for him to make contact.

She had little opportunity to brood. There was only two months to go before her exhibition, and she had lost time owing to illness. Her working days began to extend up to ten hours, and she would hardly have left her studio if Jean had not insisted she have three square meals a day with the family.

On returning from a family supper one evening, she found Steve waiting for her, having a glass of superior Bordeaux.

"Steve! How lovely to see you." She kissed him briefly on the cheek, hoping the enthusiasm in her voice did not sound too forced. After the door, she ushered him in, bustling into the kitchen on the pretext of looking for glasses. Once out of sight she leaned against the cabinets and breathed deeply, trying to calm her racing thoughts. Because of illness and work commitments, she had seen little of Steve since New Year's Eve. She knew she had to break with him but, like a coward, she had procrastinated.

It was so soon after his separation from Susannah! She hated the thought of hurting him further. Sighing, she seized two wine glasses and returned to the living room.

Steve had made himself at home, putting on some music, a light classical piece with romantic overtones. He poured a glass for Kathryn. "Cheers, love."

Kathryn drank a little wine then hovered nervously as Steve settled himself on the couch, patting the seat next to him. As she hesitated, he seized her hand, ready to pull her down beside him. To her horror, Kathryn found herself recoiling from his touch.

Steve's hand dropped to his side. "Don't worry, Kathryn, I am a gentleman."

"Oh, Steve, I'm sorry." She sat beside him, brown eyes fixed anxiously on his face. "You see . . ."

"Spare me the explanations." His tone was brusque as he turned from her, eyes focused midair. "I'm not a fool and I know things aren't right between us, never have been, really. And something happened on New Year's Eve . . ." His shoulders rose in a sad, puzzled gesture. "I don't want to pry," he added, noting her expression, "but I've known it was over since that night."

Much moved, Kathryn clasped his hands in hers. "I'm very fond of you, Steve, I really am—but it's not enough. You deserve the best—someone who really loves you."

"The mythical Miss Right?" Steve inquired bitterly.

"Not so mythical," Kathryn insisted, "and one day you'll meet her." Strange how she could be certain of Steve's future happiness while remaining unsure of her own. She picked up her wine glass. "Look, Steve, we've known each other a long time. We tried romance and it didn't work, but let's celebrate to what we do have—friendship." To her relief Steve reached for his glass, a smile dawning on his face.

By the time he left Steve was in remarkably good spirits, and Kathryn could congratulate herself on clearing the air between them while retaining a valued friendship. One aspect of her life had been sorted out, but after Steve's departure she returned to her now empty living room and was struck anew by the solitary nature of her life. It was over a week since she'd been to the Manor, and she'd heard nothing from Gerard. She hugged herself in an instinctive attempt to appease the pain of his loss, then switched off the light and went to bed.

Jean greeted the news of Steve and Kathryn's breakup with tut-tutting and knowing shakes of the head. David showed little surprise. "There was never much of a spark in that relationship, was there?" he commented over morning coffee. "I've realized that for some time. Just wondered when you would."

"Never much of a spark!" Jean repeated in disgust as she moved around the kitchen, flapping a cloth at imaginary specks of dust. "You young people expect too much. Always expecting bells to ring. You may be waiting forever!"

The door slammed shut on her homily as Kathryn and David grinned ruefully at each other over their coffee. "She's just upset," David said. "She's dying for one of us to get married and, as yet, there's nothing on the horizon."

"Talking of marriage," Kathryn said, "who's the new girlfriend?"

"What new girlfriend?" David inquired innocently.

"The one you've been out with every night this week. It's certainly not Jenny—she hasn't seen you for weeks."

"Early days yet, Kath. Nothing to report." David rose, placed his coffee mug in the dishwasher, then left, saying he had to get on with some work. Puzzled, Kathryn watched his retreating back. What was all the secrecy about? Shaking her head she finished her coffee, concluding wryly that she'd never get a grip on her cousin's varied love life.

Next morning, as she was riding Jasper past the Manor, Douglas Talbot stopped in his limousine and told her he had just managed to get a message through to Gerard's staff. He'd no doubt that Gerard would be contacting her shortly. Thanking him warmly, it occurred to her that her pessimism regarding his silence had been premature and, as she went on her way, she, mentally rehearsed what she would say to him when they finally spoke. She knew that her words would be crucial as she would not get a second chance.

She need not have worried. As the raw days of February closed in, there was deafening silence from across the Atlantic, and Kathryn came to the reluctant conclusion that Gerard wanted nothing further to do with her.

The somber weather matched her mood. A relatively mild January had given way to north easterly gales and freezing mists, as Hollinswood Stables was thrust suddenly into winter at its worst. Most riding lessons were cancelled because of hazardous conditions, and just caring for the stabled horses and the native ponies who were still out in the paddocks became a full-time job. They had to take each day as it came, often dealing with unexpected emergencies, and when the water pipe supplying the loose boxes ruptured, it was Kathryn and David who effected a temporary repair until the plumber could negotiate the icy road conditions to reach them.

Harry's condition deteriorated sharply with the harsh weather, and when snow set in, he had to retreat, reluctantly, to the house. Kathryn stepped in, and her days began at six in the morning as she struggled through drifts to transport hay and pony nuts on foot to their native ponies who clustered together in desolate, wind-lashed fields beside dry stone walls banked high with snow.

Snowplows turned the lanes into single tracks, but further snow falls often undermined their work. Douglas Talbot earned the villagers' gratitude by hiring a snowplow whose sole purpose was to clear the lanes running in and out of the village.

After a hard day battling with the elements, Kathryn would often collapse, exhausted, into bed, grateful that she had no time or energy to brood on her love life.

The thaw was slow and uneven, but the beginning of March saw a sudden mild spell that turned the fields into quagmires and swelled the streams as the snow melted with unexpected speed.

Kathryn's mood lightened. It was time to thrust her personal problems aside and focus on her career. Her exhibition was only three weeks away, and she had to make important decisions on how to present her work. On reflection, it seemed logical to group all her local landscapes along seasonal lines, highlighting the contrasting shades and timbres of northern scenery throughout the year. Her French landscapes, with stronger colors dictating a bolder style, could form a separate category. Kathryn took a selection of her paintings to the gallery to try out her ideas *in situ* and recruited Steve as her helper, finding his down-to-earth comments useful as she tried out different hanging arrangements. She had been relieved to find that they could still see each other on a friendly, casual basis, and now that there was no romantic pressure on her, she enjoyed their outings all the more.

With the arrival of warmer weather, Harry's health improved and his return to work freed Kathryn from stable duties and relieved Jean of his grumpy presence in the house. Spirits in the Robertson family rose further when Harry received a message to visit the Manor in order to discuss the land situation.

Kathryn found it difficult to concentrate on work on the afternoon of her uncle's appointment. In the end she downed tools and joined Jean in an anxious vigil around the kitchen table. Harry returned when they were on their second cup of tea and threw a legal-looking document down on the table.

"Signed, sealed, and delivered." He drew a chair up, looking from his wife to his niece. "We have a lease for all our paddocks, at a very low rent. There's only one problem."

"Problem?" Jean's voice rose.

"Afraid so," Harry replied. "It's only for one year."

"A year!" Kathryn put in. "Why?"

Harry's brow wrinkled. "Douglas Talbot explained it all, but most of it was as clear as mud. Apparently, as Lady Alice left her affairs in a terrible mess, the lawyers are still trying to sort everything out. Talbot thought we'd prefer this temporary lease as an interim measure."

"And in a year's time?" asked Jean.

"We get our long-term lease. Talbot promised me that." Harry patted his wife's hand. "Don't worry, lass. It'll sort itself out."

Kathryn hoped so, wondering not for the first time if they could trust the people up at the Manor. She had fallen in love with Gerard, but what did she really know about him? He headed a large company and made decisions every day that could make or break whole communities. What did a small number of people in a remote part of England matter? What could one woman matter? She shivered, cupping her hot mug with her hands for warmth.

The opening of Kathryn's exhibition was imminent. She was at the gallery most evenings, ironing out hitches and arranging and rearranging the paintings, often succumbing to last-minute panic as she convinced herself that she could be in for a public humiliation.

The opening day found her in a much calmer frame of mind as, with the director of the gallery at her side, she greeted newspaper journalists. They were keen to ask her searching questions and she was doing her best to answer them when she became vaguely aware that what seemed like the whole population of Hollinswood was pouring into the tiny gallery. She offered up a silent prayer of thanksgiving for the loyalty of friends and family, then set off to reach Harry and Jean at the far side of the room.

"Miss Beaumont?"

"Yes." Kathryn turned at the sound of a soft American accent to find a tall striking-looking woman at her shoulder. Reddish brown hair shaped into a gleaming bob framed an oval face marked by strong features and black arching eyebrows. Kathryn knew who she was before she introduced herself.

"Hi, I'm Marsha Fitzalan, and I just wanted to come over and say how much I'm enjoying your exhibition."

"Thank you." Kathryn smiled, genuinely pleased by the older woman's appreciation.

"I guess we're neighbors, in a way. Douglas tells me you live virtually next door to Hollinswood Manor—and I guess you know who I am by my name."

"Of course. Are you staying in the neighborhood for long?"

"Not long enough. I decided to come over and check out the Manor. Why, it's beautiful, and so is the setting. We've made a wise purchase. However," she added, her tone becoming brisker, "I really wanted to talk to you about your landscapes, which I adore. Do you paint outdoors or in the studio?"

"Outdoors, *in situ*, preferably. Because our climate is so variable, I always make detailed notes of colors and weather conditions. I also use photography to capture a certain moment in time—then pictures can be completed indoors if I'm in a rush to meet a deadline."

Marsha stepped aside to scrutinize a picture of moorland under a grainy sky streaked with linear cloud formations. "You certainly have the gift of portraying upland scenery," she commented, her next query taking Kathryn by surprise. "You accept commissions, I take it?"

"Of course, when I can get them." Kathryn smiled ruefully. "Usually I paint first and hope to sell afterward."

"Then perhaps you'll hear from me." She shook hands with a firm grip and Kathryn watched surreptitiously as Marsha rejoined a group from the Manor headed by Douglas Talbot.

So that was Gerard's mother—no wonder he had such strength of character! Her encounter with Marsha had been brief but revealing. There was a lady who knew her own mind, a lady who would always get what she wanted. And Gerard—what did he want? Not Kathryn, that was for sure; his resounding silence had spoken louder than words.

Chapter Seven

In the following week Kathryn basked in the glow of professional success. Sales at the exhibition were healthy, and the gallery owner was clearly pleased that his gamble in backing a little-known artist had paid off. One or two London-based galleries expressed an interest in her work, but Kathryn knew it would be some time before she could rely on an outlet in the capital. She began to experience a feeling of anticlimax, uncertain what steps to take next to promote her fledgling career. In this hiatus she was pleased when Marsha Fitzalan rang and asked to meet for lunch to discuss a commission.

"Thanks for agreeing to meet me, Miss Beaumont." Marsha raised her glass of mineral water toward Kathryn in a friendly gesture.

"Thank you for asking me, Mrs. Fitzalan."

"Please, call me Marsha."

"Please, call me Kathryn," Kathryn echoed, and both women laughed.

They were in a Buxton hotel and at that moment a waiter arrived with the menus. Kathryn chose Dover sole then leaned back, curious to know what her companion had to say. Marsha placed her order and sent the waiter off, then looked across at Kathryn with one of her disconcertingly direct stares.

"Let's get down to business. I was impressed with your exhibition and I'd like to commission you to paint a series of landscapes of Connemara scenery. To be hung in Fitzalan House, our family home. I would, of course, offer you full hospitality while you were working on the project."

"I see." Kathryn's hand tightened on the water glass as she attempted to school her features into a neutral mask. She felt as though Marsha had handed her a smoking bomb, for how could she allow herself to be whisked off to Ireland—to Gerard's family home? At the same time her blood rose at the thought of the professional challenge, of a commission from a woman who could afford to hire a well-known artist but had chosen her. It could do her career a lot of good. But she needed to know more before she could make a decision. "How many paintings do you envisage?" she asked. "And how long would I have to stay? I wouldn't want to put you out at all."

"Oh, you wouldn't be putting me out," returned Marsha quickly. "To be honest I'd be glad of the company as my son, Gerard, is too busy running the family business to visit often and our nearest neighbor is some miles away. As to the length of your stay, I'm not sure how many paintings I require yet. I thought we'd sort that out when you arrived."

Assuming I arrive at all, Kathryn thought, though Marsha had told her what she needed to know— Gerard would not be there.

"You would have full artistic control," Marsha went on, sensing Kathryn's hesitation, "and my terms would be most generous."

She was really making it most difficult to refuse. "When would you want me to start?" Kathryn asked.

"Well, let's see now. I return home next week and have a few things to attend to. April's good for me. How about you?"

Kathryn had to admit she had nothing organized in the near future. Spring and summer stretched emptily before her, with few personal or professional events to look forward to. She really would be a fool to turn down such a lucrative and prestigious contract. "I'd be delighted to accept your commission," she said, with a fervent wish that she would not have cause to regret her decision.

"Kathryn, that's just great! You'll be itching to get those watercolors out as soon as you see our mountains and lakes. And we'll make you real welcome at Fitzalan House—you'll fall in love with the whole place, just you see."

I fell in love with its owner, Kathryn thought forlornly, reaching forward to grasp Marsha's proffered hand. Smiling into Marsha's eyes, she had a fleeting moment of panic which she squashed immediately. She would only come across Gerard in photographs and conversation, and she could handle that, she was sure of it.

Kathryn landed at Galway airport one cool evening in early April. She only had a small suitcase to deal with, having sent on her painting equipment, and had little difficulty in locating the driver sent to meet her, a garrulous young man named William. Traveling northwest from Galway along a deserted main road, William seemed content to carry on a one-sided conversation while she concentrated on drinking in the scenery. It looked like a landscape from a child's painting, the brilliant green daubed on in thick strokes, the turf dotted with whitewashed cottages gleaming in the last rays of the setting sun. The pewter-colored stone walls dissecting the land reminded Kathryn of home, but everything else had a starkness and melancholy beauty that seemed unique to this area.

She was unaware of time passing, and when a mountain range rose in view on their left, she was surprised when William announced they were almost there. Within fifteen minutes the car made a sharp right turn onto a narrow lane enfolded by deciduous trees, their thick branches interwoven to form a long dark tunnel. They took another lurch to the right and, unexpectedly, light hit the inside of the car as the trees were left behind and Kathryn found herself staring across the dark gray waters of a small lake which bordered the road on the left-hand side, its gleaming surface undisturbed by wind or rain.

"Quite a sheltered spot," William remarked, pointing to the wooded escarpments that encircled the lake. "Hills keep out the worst of the weather. And that's Fitzalan House," he added, "coming up on our right."

Kathryn was silent, lost in contemplation of the Fitzalan home, which seemed to grow out of the very hillside. Built out of large chunks of iron gray-stone, with square towers, turrets, and castellated walls, it appeared to have been transported to this lonely spot from an illustration in a book of fairy tales.

"Here we are, Miss." The car came to a halt and the studded wooden door opened, the outdoor light outlining Marsha's figure as she came to greet them. She took Kathryn's bag, thanked William, and then drew Kathryn inside.

Kathryn stepped into a large, square hallway with

a stone-flagged floor and walls paneled in dark oak heavily decorated with medieval armory. What she assumed to be the Fitzalan family crest had been carved into the stone mantel of the fireplace, which dominated the opposite wall and stood to the right of the broad staircase.

Marsha echoed Kathryn's thoughts. "It's a bit of a mausoleum, isn't it?"

Kathryn turned to her hostess in confusion. "Oh, no, it's very . . . er . . . impressive. And I'm really glad to be here," she added in a rush.

"I'm glad to hear it. But there's no need to be polite." She waved a hand around the hallway. "This place is not as ancient as it appears. One of the mad Fitzalans, who had pretensions to being a medieval baron, built it in the eighteen sixties. Knocked a perfectly good house down to make way for it. But"—she shrugged her shoulders in resignation—"it's the family home and I do my best to look after it." She turned toward her guest, drawing an arm through hers. "Come into the parlor, I've got refreshments waiting."

Marsha led her into a small, square room cosily furnished with a log fire blazing brightly in the hearth. Kathryn breathed in the scented wood smoke appreciatively. "Mmm—applewood."

Marsha drew a chintz-covered armchair forward and set out a small round table with coffee and sandwiches. Kathryn ate well; the insubstantial snack she had received on the plane had hardly blunted her appetite, and as she demolished the sandwiches, she found herself able to talk to Marsha with the ease of an old friend. By the time she finished eating, her eyelids were drooping and she was finding it difficult to concentrate on her words.

Marsha noticed. "I'll take you to your room now," she said kindly. "You've had a very long journey." She led Kathryn to the first floor and into a room furnished in a surprisingly contemporary fashion, with curtains and bedcovers in a vibrant flowery material, cream walls, and pine bedroom furniture.

"I do hope you like your room. It's in the wing that I'm modernizing, as fast as my traditionalist son will allow, anyway."

Kathryn expressed delight. Then Marsha left, and she showered and then curled up in the substantial bed. She could unpack in the morning, she decided, happy to lose herself in a deep and dreamless sleep.

She woke late next morning to find an elderly woman placing a tea tray beside her. "The mist is down," she declared, her brogue strong and her pale blue eyes kind. "But it'll lift before morning. Come to the kitchen when you're ready, me dear. I'm Annie, by the way." She stumped off, leaving Kathryn to hurry to the window, push the casement wide open, and gaze at the thick white mist that wreathed the house like a pearl choker.

After unpacking and dressing she went downstairs and made her way to the kitchen. The old lady who had served the tea was bustling around. "Morning, dearie." She acknowledged Kathryn with a lopsided grin. "Sit yourself down. I've got your breakfast all ready."

"Thank you, Annie." Kathryn balked at the size of the cooked breakfast placed in front of her, but once she started she found her appetite keen. Annie bustled and chattered and Kathryn learned a good deal in a short space of time. Annie worked daily, returning home after the evening meal had been cooked, and had worked for the Fitzalans for years—before "Young Gerard" had been born. Talking of the family with a proprietary air, it was Annie's considered opinion that Gerard should visit his mother more often. "There again, the lad was devastated when his father died." Annie tut-tutted, shaking her head. "Daresay this house reminds him too much of the past—the poor lamb." Kathryn almost choked on her bacon hearing Gerard referred to as a lamb. Yet Annie had revealed one important fact: It was unlikely that Gerard would pay even a fleeting visit during her stay. To her surprise, and dismay, a keening disappointment washed over her. Was this really why she had come—a secret wish to rekindle a flame? If so, she was crazy. She shook herself mentally. She must give up hope of Gerard once and for all, for only then could she build up a happy life for herself.

"Morning." Marsha, framed in the doorway, looked neat and fresh in cream linen snacks and a cornflower blue cotton blouse. She took the cup of coffee offered by Annie and joined Kathryn at the table. "I see you've received one of Annie's royal breakfasts. You're honored." She exchanged amused glances with the old lady, then drained her cup placing it back on the table with a flourish. "If you've finished, Kathryn, I'll show you round."

As they walked and talked through passageways that all looked the same Kathryn had to admit that Marsha's joking reference to the place as a mausoleum was fairly accurate. The house had been modeled along the lines of a medieval fortress, and the paneled corridors, ancestral portraits, and military memorabilia created a rather oppressive atmosphere.

"My husband wouldn't hear of any changes," Marsha confided, "but since he died I've started to modernize parts of the house. Gerard wasn't too keen at first but I've brought him around. He likes what I've done in here, anyway." The door swung open and Kathryn stepped into a large, rectangular-shaped room carpeted in pale green and filled with two chunky couches in ivory-colored leather at right angles to each other. Freestanding bookshelves in pale wood, stacked high with hard-backed books in bright dust jackets, broke up the cream walls, and the floor space was dotted with small, round tables clothed in linen and lace tablecloths and laden with family photographs in silver filigree frames. Gerard's face, from boyhood to present day, leaped out at her. "Charming," she breathed, then tore her eyes away from his features.

"I intend to hang your landscapes in here," Marsha said. "This room is my own private haven, and I want to add some interest and color."

Kathryn assessed the wall space. "There's plenty of room and the background color is neutral. It's an ideal hanging space," she concluded with satisfaction, then turned to her hostess. "What we need to do now is work out exactly which views you want me to paint."

"I'd like you to start close to home first," Marsha explained. "I think we should take some local walks, look at the house from different angles, then decide." She crossed to the wide windows and Kathryn followed her. The mist had cleared with startling suddenness, and the sun was beginning to break through gray-tinged ragged clouds. In front of them a series of blue-gray mountains, edged by sunlight, reached skyward, mountaintops obscured by wispy cloud formations. The breath caught in Kathryn's throat; this was a landscape artist's paradise.

Marsha's words echoed her thoughts. "It's a bright and glorious day, Kathryn. Shall we begin?"

Over the next week she and Marsha walked and talked, explored the local vicinity, then traveled into Connermara National Park to take in the varied scenery, from large lakes to open moorland, where herds of wild ponies roamed. Marsha was engaging company and she had firm ideas on what she wanted. They weighed up the merits of various locations and finally decided on a series of eight medium-sized landscapes showing different aspects of Connermara scenery.

The commission would keep Kathryn at Fitzalan House for some time, and she didn't know whether that was a good or bad thing. The change of scene was doing her good, she enjoyed Marsha's company, and she loved the area . . . but . . . at Fitzalan House Gerard's presence was everywhere, from childhood books named in a rounded, careful script, to photograph albums recording his progress from coltish youth to the mature, self-confident man who had caused such havoc in her life. It was a sobering experience looking at current photographs of Gerard. Many were taken at New York social functions, and rarely was he seen with the same woman twice. From blondes to brunettes, they all exuded the same qualities of metropolitan glamour.

Marsha's frequent comments added to the picture

Kathryn was building up of Gerard's private life. He was too addicted to glitzy airheads, his mother would often declare, too concerned with finding the right escort for the right social occasion than with forming deeper bonds. Kathryn would listen to these forthright opinions in uncomfortable silence, her sense of inadequacy reinforced as she contemplated the futility of her own tentative ambitions in that direction. It was time to drop her own romantic illusions, she often reminded herself, and accept reality—even though it was a cold and lonely condition.

She began her first painting, a view of Fitzalan House from the hillside to the southeast, with views of the blue ridge mountains of the Twelve Pins as a backdrop. This was a professional challenge she was going to enjoy, she decided, as she began her preliminary sketch in charcoal. Her fingers flew across the paper, and once the rough outline was completed, she made detailed color notes. Marsha had placed a room at her disposal for a studio, but she intended to do as much work outside as possible. Over the next few days she worked long hours, returning only when light began to fade to share a late supper with Marsha.

One evening, toward the end of the second week of her visit, Kathryn returned earlier than usual, driven indoors by dark clouds and ominous rumblings of thunder, to find Marsha's sitting room empty. The house seemed unnaturally quiet, and driven by a sense of unease, Kathryn made her way upstairs to Marsha's bedroom. A groan reached her ears as she reached the top of the stairs and Kathryn raced along the corridor in record time to come to a sudden halt at the open bedroom door.

Marsha, her back facing the door, was slumped across her dressing table. She stirred and turned her head on Kathryn's approach, and Kathryn's heart jumped in fear at the sight of her ashen face. "Kathryn—thank heaven." Her breathing was labored as she drew one hand across her chest and managed to utter one word: "Pain."

Kathryn moved across to her swiftly, placed an arm around her shoulders and looked into her anxious eyes. "Don't try to speak, Marsha. I'll phone for an ambulance."

There was a phone by the bedside and Kathryn rang 999, thankful that emergency procedures were the same as in Britain. She was put through to medical services and gave details, requesting an ambulance. "Please hurry," she said, lowering her voice to a whisper. "I think it may be a heart attack."

On replacing the receiver she moved into Marsha's bathroom and began a feverish search through the cabinet in there. Her medical knowledge was rudimentary but she knew that aspirin dispensed to a heart patient might mean the difference between life and death. Thank goodness! Her hand closed over a full bottle of aspirin, and she filled a glass with water and returned to Marsha's side. "Chew two tablets," she advised, "then drink some water." Marsha complied, and Kathryn returned to the bathroom to rinse a washcloth in warm water and collect a towel.

She made Marsha comfortable with extra cushions, then wiped her face and hands free of perspiration, drying them on the warm, fluffy towel. Marsha made no attempt to speak but her breathing seemed easier and her color less ghastly as Kathryn finished her ministrations. "The ambulance will be here soon," she said, taking Marsha's hand reassuringly. "And they'll take good care of you."

The ambulance was, indeed, remarkably quick, and Kathryn stood aside, happy to relinquish responsibility as efficient paramedics settled Marsha into the emergency vehicle. She made arrangements to follow on in Marsha's car, and as the ambulance, lights flashing, hurtled off into the gathering gloom of a stormy night, Kathryn set off at a more sedate pace. As directed, she took the Clifden road branching off to the southeast of the market town and, with little traffic, she made good progress, drawing into the hospital parking lot only half an hour after leaving Fitzalan House.

Hurried inquiries took her to an empty waiting room, where a charming nurse brought her a cup of tea. She flicked through magazines in a desultory fashion, eyes turning frequently to her watch, as minutes turned into one hour, then two.

The door opened, startling her out of her reverie, and a broad, beefy-looking man in a white coate bore down on her, hand outstretched. "Miss Beaumont, I believe. I'm Doctor Hennessy. I'm dealing with Mrs. Fitzalan's case."

"How is she, Doctor?" Kathryn asked, shaking his hand.

"Out of danger." Kathryn exhaled, aware of a sudden release of tension. "It was a heart attack," the doctor went on, "but it appears to have been a mild one, and her condition has stabilized. Your prompt action in calling for help and dispensing aspirin is much appreciated, and Mrs. Fitzalan asked me to pass on her thanks."

"I'm just glad I could help." Kathryn bit her lip, a brief glimpse of Gerard flashing before her eyes. "Now that I have definite news, I really must contact her family."

"Done." A grin crossed Doctor Hennessy's broad face. "Don't look so surprised, Miss Beaumont, we're a small community, we know everyone's business. Admin has been on to the Fitzalan lawyer in Clifden. He'll get a message through to that globe-trotting son of hers." So, she wouldn't even have to speak to Gerard on the phone. "You go home and rest now. There's nothing more you can do—contact us in the morning."

Kathryn thanked the doctor and then left, relieved that she only had a short distance to drive. As she entered the empty house she was hit by exhaustion and a sudden realization that she'd eaten nothing all evening. She prepared sandwiches and hot milk, took her meal up to her room, and ate there. She felt emotionally drained. Seeing Marsha doubled up in pain had been a traumatic experience, and she switched off her lamp and settled down to sleep with some relief.

Through an uneasy slumber broken by disturbing dream images she was dimly aware of being dragged reluctantly into consciousness. She opened her eyes cautiously, knowing by the blackness that it was dead of night and, by the soft sounds creeping up from downstairs that someone else was in the house. The luminous hands of the clock told her it was three thirty. She switched the lamp on and slithered from the bed, shivering in her short, silk shift as her feet touched the floor and the doctor's words echoed in her mind: "We're a small community, we know everyone's business." Had some lowlife come to help himself, expecting the house to be empty?

They had reckoned without her and there was no way she was going to let Fitzalan House be burgled while she was in charge of it! Frantically she glanced around for a suitable weapon, then seized one of the tall, brass candlesticks adorning the mantelpiece. She brandished it in her right hand, heavy base uppermost. Slipping on her robe, she made little noise in her bare feet as she made her way downstairs, pausing at regular intervals to listen. There was complete silence.

The sounds seemed to have emanated from the kitchen area, so she decided to investigate there first. Pausing in the open doorway, she peered cautiously into the room. It was empty and lit by the amber glow of the central light that hung low over the huge scrubbed pine table in the center of the room. It looked untouched, normal—yet she was sure she'd switched the light off. Was she dreaming? Had the upsets of the evening unhinged her brain? She stepped gingerly into the room, her palms moist and the fine hair on the back of her neck prickling. In spite of the normality of the scene she could not shake off the feeling that she was not alone. Her heightened senses picked up a faint sound and she whipped round as the door of the wine cellar opened behind her. The blood thudded in her ears as she brandished the candlestick above her head ready to rain blows on the tall man now stepping into the room.

Chapter Eight

"Kathryn!" Strong fingers curled around her right wrist, forcing her fingers open so that the candlestick fell on to the floor with a heavy thud. She tried to scream but no words would come as her other wrist was seized and held in front of her. "Kathryn, it's me—Gerard." The words penetrated her bemused brain and she looked up into a face long dreamed of, now made flesh.

"Gerard," she said dully, the words stumbling from her. "It can't be . . . how did you get here so quickly?"

"Simple—I was already in Ireland on business." He was still holding her wrists with bruising intensity, as though unwilling to relinquish his hold. "When the message reached me I drove straight here. I've just returned from the hospital."

"In time to give me an awful fright." She flung

the words at him in a breathless rush. "I thought you were a burglar . . ." Her voice choked and next moment she was pulled, unresisting, into his arms and he was murmuring soft reassurances, her head resting beneath his chin as though they had never been apart. The scent of his spicy aftershave enveloped her as she nestled against him and gave way to emotions that had threatened to engulf her ever since she had found Marsha in pain.

The storm of weeping began to subside, but his arms stayed around her, one hand stroking the curls back from her forehead while he gently rocked her from side to side. It felt so good to be in his arms again. She lifted her face to his, lips parting, wide brown eyes washed bright by tears.

His eyes burned into hers, then, as though fearful of what they might reveal. He released her, turning away with the words, "Sit yourself down, Kate, and I'll make coffee."

When he joined her at the table she realized with a sudden shock that he looked quite dreadful. His black turtleneck sweater emphasized the paleness of his face, and the stark electric light picked out the smudges beneath his eyes. Stubble was already beginning to shadow his chin, and strain was etched into every feature. Her heart turned over with sympathy. His father had died of a sudden heart attack and now his mother had been threatened by the same fate. Kathryn took the drink offered, resisting the impulse to cover his hand with hers. Instead she said, "Your mother will be all right, you know."

"The doctors seem quite confident she's out of danger." He grimaced slightly, his hair flopping forward in glossy strands across his forehead. "It's been a darned shock. She's always been so fit, a real powerhouse of a woman."

"And will be again," Kathryn insisted. "I'm sure she'll make a complete recovery."

"Well, I'll have you thank if she does. The doctors told me how well you acted."

"I did the best I could." Her lashes shadowed her cheeks as she began to drink slowly from her mug as the silence stretched out between them.

"You've got a lot of guts, Kathryn," he said suddenly. "Not many people would react so calmly to a medical emergency or be prepared to tackle a suspected intruder. I can't begin to tell you how grateful I am."

Color etched her cheeks and, eager to retain the sudden warmth that had sprung up between them, she was about to say more when he surprised her by standing up and saying, "I've disrupted your sleep for long enough. I'll bid you good night, Kathryn."

She murmured a response and then tracked his retreating form with curious eyes before following in his footsteps.

* * *

The next morning Kathryn woke, heavy-eyed, to find that she had slept late. She hurried downstairs to find Annie alone in the kitchen struggling to come to terms with the momentous events of the night before. Stress seemed to be taking her to new heights with the frying pan. "The missus has had a good night," she said, placing a gigantic breakfast in front of Kathryn. "Gerard's just phoned from the hospital. He went there straight after breakfast. Said to leave you to sleep in—oh, and he'll see you at lunch."

Annie's chatter drifted over her as she took in this new piece of information. Relieved to hear of Marsha's good progress Kathryn decided to while away the time until lunch by walking in the wooded countryside around Fitzalan House. After all, there was little point in continuing her work until she knew what was to happen to the commission.

She returned at midday, hot and sticky from her exertions and from the unseasonably warm weather which had suddenly visited this part of Ireland. An hour later, showered and dressed in a cotton shift in pale lilac, she was directed by Annie towards the Conservatory which had been built on to the sunny southwest corner of the house.

Gerard was standing at the table, tossing the salad in a wooden bowl. Dressed in cream slacks and a short-sleeved shirt in crisp green cotton, his features relaxed and his movements free of tension, he seemed very different from the man she had encountered last night. He looked up at her approach and she received the full impact of his devastating smile. "Kate! Good afternoon. Sit down and enjoy Annie's delicious lunch."

He had called her Kate! The use of this warm and very personal diminutive seemed symbolic of the new warmth that was springing up between them, and as she helped herself to cold chicken and salad and poured herself a glass of sparkling grape juice, she couldn't help wondering if a new beginning might be possible for them.

The first priority, though, was Marsha, and as they settled down to eat she inquired after her.

"She's a marvel," Gerard declared. "She's already sitting up in bed, bossing everyone around and chafing at her inactivity."

"I'm so pleased." The sun's rays slanted through the half-drawn blinds to bathe Gerard's head and shoulders in a soft light and pick out the reddish strands of his hair. His glance embraced her like a warm summer shower, and she had to fight a sudden, crazy impulse to blurt out her feelings for him. Shakily she picked up her fork, her eyes firmly on her plate, and began to eat.

Her appetite blunted, Kathryn pushed her plate away from her and broke the companionable silence. "I'm looking forward to seeing Marsha," she remarked. "When will she be coming home?"

"She'll be released for respite care tomorrow, but she won't be coming home." Kathryn's brows rose in surprise as Gerard continued, "I've arranged for her to go to a nursing home, where she can have constant care. This place is too isolated to attract the right kind of help."

"How long will she be away?" Kathryn asked.

"I've no idea. That will depend on the medical staff."

"I see." If Marsha was not returning home, she really must clarify her own position. Was she to stay and paint—or go? She opened her mouth to speak only to be interrupted by the sharp ringing of the telephone. Gerard went to answer it, and after a few muffled words turned toward her. "It's for you, Kathryn—Steve Barrington."

Why on earth was Steve phoning her? Thoughts of disasters at Hollinswood Stables shot through her mind, and she hurried to the phone, stomach muscles clenching.

Steve's tone of voice immediately reassured her. Her name "Kathryn!" fairly bubbled along the line. "I've got wonderful news for you," he went on breathlessly. "Susannah and I are back together, and she's agreed to become my wife!"

"Steve, I'm so pleased." He deserved his good fortune, he really did.

"I wanted you to be one of the first to know—after all, you've been a great friend to me, seeing me through a really bad patch. I don't know how I'd have managed without you, Kath."

"Oh, Steve . . ." His words brought a glow to her cheeks, such appreciation from an old friend meaning a great deal to her. The sound of a glass breaking and a muffled curse behind her cut into her thoughts. "Look, Steve, I'll have to go now," she muttered hurriedly, "but I'm glad you rang."

"Okay, Kath, but don't forget you're guest of honor at our wedding in August."

"I can't wait," Kathryn laughed. "Bye for now." She replaced the receiver and turned to find Gerard sweeping up the fragments of a broken glass.

"You look pleased, Kathryn. Good news from Hollinswood?"

"Oh, yes, Steve—"

"Ah, young Barrington. He's well I take it?"

"He certainly is, in fact he rang with special news. He's—"

"No need to discuss your private affairs with me," Gerard cut in smoothly, his mouth twisting in derision. "After all you'll be able to discuss this 'special news' in person soon enough."

What did he mean? He spoke as though her departure to Hollinswood was imminent. She surveyed him surreptitiously, his expression shuttered as though once more he was intent on freezing her out. Was she to be subjected once more to one of his quixotic change of moods? "So," she said thinly, "you want me to return to Hollinswood?"

"That would be for the best." His jawline tightened as he continued, "I have to return to the States soon. Fitzalan House will be empty."

And I might steal the family silver if I stay unsupervised, Kathryn thought angrily. Aloud she said, "When am I to go?"

"If you could pack this afternoon I could get you to the airport tonight."

So soon? She was to bundled out of the house like unwanted garbage. Keep a hold over your temper, she warned herself. Don't let him have the satisfaction of knowing how rattled you are. "What about the commission?" she asked levelly.

"I'm sure my mother will be in touch as soon as she's fully recovered," he returned. "In the meantime if you'd care to submit a bill for expenses incurred to Hollinswood Manor, I'll make sure the staff deals with it promptly."

That was the final straw. "The Manor will see no bill from me." She rose, brown eyes blazing. "Your mother has given me a wonderful holiday. That's reward enough for me. Now I must go and pack."

Kathryn repacked her case for the third time then sat forlornly on the bed wondering what time she would be leaving. She glanced at her painting equipment stacked and ready to be sent on separately, the unfinished painting in her portfolio a sad reminder of her time here.

Annie brought tea at four o'clock with surprising news. "Gerard's gone to the hospital," she announced. "The missus is to be released early, and he's taking her to the nursing home." The lines on Annie's face deepened as her face broke into a smile. "And you're to stay another night, me darlin'. Gerard won't be able to take you to the airport until tomorrow now." She leaned over Kathryn like a mother hen over a favorite chick. "I'll leave you a lovely supper—one of your favorites."

Much moved, Kathryn hugged the old lady. At least someone would be sorry to see her leave Fitzalan House!

Kathryn completed her light makeup, then slipped into an elegant black, ankle-length column dress, split up one side to mid-thigh. Although she was dining alone, she took great pains with her appearance, determined to spend her last evening at Fitzalan House in some style! The grandfather clock began to chime eight o'clock, and she slipped on her shoes and hurried downstairs.

It was still unseasonably warm and Kathryn brushed her curls back from her forehead as she entered the dining room, her hand poising in midair at the sight of Gerard's tall figure at the sideboard, coolly ladling out soup from the heated container.

He turned at her approach. "Ah, Kathryn, I assumed you'd be on time." In deference to the warm weather he was wearing a lightweight suit in ivory, light brown tie, and cream shirt. Kathryn's first feeling of relief that she had made herself presentable was quickly followed by panic. He wasn't supposed to be here, her mind shrieked. Annie had assured her he would stay overnight at the nursing home. Why had he returned?

She lowered herself into her chair and began to eat Annie's delicious mushroom soup and homemade rolls, which could have been clear water and sawdust for all she cared; her appetite was as jangled as her nerves. She made an effort to break the silence that bristled between them. "I do hope your mother is well."

He spoke as if reading a news bulletin. "She's comfortable—and happy with the nursing home, thank you."

Thank you for nothing, Kathryn thought sourly. Remember, this is the man who is throwing you out, she warned herself, uneasily aware that every moment he made, from the elegant flick of the wrist as he upturned his wine glass to the way he sipped his soup was causing her pulse to race in a crazy fashion. Why hadn't he stayed away! "You're not staying at the nursing home tonight, then?" she said, her thoughts translating abruptly into speech.

"Obviously not." Gerard's dry comment was accompanied by a wolfish grin which showed the sharp edges of his white, even teeth. "Why? Are you nervous at the prospect of spending the evening with me?"

"No."

"Only I wouldn't like to put temptation in your way," he continued silkily.

"Believe me," Kathryn snapped, "there would be no temptation."

"I'm glad to hear it," he returned. "I wouldn't want the little boyfriend—the boy next door—to get jealous."

Kathryn drew a deep breath. In his careless, insolent way Gerard was trying to provoke and patronize her, to get beneath her skin making snide insinuations. The truth might be the best weapon against him.

"For what it's worth," she said, "Steve Barrington is not my boyfriend."

"Oh, yes?" Now he was openly sneering. "Then why did he ring you only today to breathe sweet nothings down the line?"

"If you'd let me finish one sentence this afternoon you would have found out why," Kathryn returned. Was this what Gerard's hostility was all about? An innocuous phone call from an old friend? "Steve wanted to tell me he was getting married." She enjoyed the effect of her broadside as Gerard's expression locked into disbelief. She followed up her advantage, smiling sweetly. "Naturally, I gave him my blessing. He's marrying someone he's been in love with for a long time. Steve and I finished our relationship, such as it was, in January."

"Such as it was," Gerard repeated slowly, a speculative gleam in his eyes.

She knew it was time to clear the air. After all, he was sending her packing; she'd never see him after tomorrow, so it didn't really matter what she said. "If you want it spelled out," she went on wearily, "there was never anything serious between us. We were simply old friends who enjoyed going out together."

Gerard glanced down at his wine, his brows knitting and his tone of voice dangerously even. "That's not the impression you gave me on New Year's Eve."

"It was you who jumped to conclusions," she pointed out. "I didn't put you straight because I didn't think it was any of your business. Then later, well . . ." Cheeks coloring, she attempted to put her feelings into words. "You wouldn't listen to me."

He stood up abruptly and began to pace away from her. "I was hardly in the mood for a long discourse, Kathryn. One moment you were in my arms and the next you were running back to Steve!"

She rose and left the table, squaring up to the implacable figure who stood before her. "I'm not proud of the way I behaved. Things got out of hand between us before I realized what was happening.

When I heard the clock chimes it brought me to my senses. I knew that Steve would come looking for me, and although I had not made a commitment to him, I couldn't humiliate him by letting him find me with someone else."

"So you humiliated me instead."

She flinched before the force of his anger. "I never intended to do so. I tried to explain my feelings, but you didn't give me chance."

"If you'd had a chance—all those months ago—what would you have said?"

It was the opportunity she had been waiting for, but now that the moment had arrived, she found herself swallowing nervously. "I . . . I would have told you that Steve and I were not dating and that I knew that we never could be."

"And what prompted this bout of self-knowledge?"

Was he going to make her spell it out?

"Tell me, Kathryn, I want to hear you say it."

"I realized I loved you!" She could hardly believe she had been so frank—she who had always been so reserved. She turned away in misery. What on earth would he think of her? She'd put them both in a very awkward position. It took a moment for her fraught senses to take in what she was hearing before she realized what the sounds behind her were.

"You're laughing!" She spun round with an accusatory stare to find a broad smile lighting his features.

"I'm sorry, darling. It's just that you made that sound like a terrible admission—not the most wonderful thing I've ever heard!"

Was it a wonderful thing? Kathryn looked at him suspiciously, still uncertain of his reaction.

"Don't look at me like a wounded fawn, Kate . . . Oh, my love . . ." With a few strides he was by her side, and she found herself swung high into the air. He carried her to the large, comfortable couch and sat down, cradling her in his arms.

She twined her arms around his neck and looked directly into gray eyes brimming with love. "I adore you, Kate," he growled. "I think I fell in love with you the moment you fell into my arms all those months ago. I wanted to hold on to you forever." A grim smile crossed his face. "But it wasn't to be. You had more spikes than a porcupine on battle alert. Why did you fight so hard against me, darling?"

"I was attracted to you but I didn't trust you," she told him bluntly. "You inhabited a world very different from mine and you reminded me of—"

"Of some guy who treated you badly?" he asked.

"Yes, of my ex-fiancé, Vincente, who was a liar and a cheat."

Gerard let out a long sigh. "And this Vincente," he said, eyes shifting from hers. "Do you still care for him?"

"Oh, no! Not at all!"

"Thank heavens for that." He lowered his head, his breath ruffling her curls as his warm lips made contact with her forehead. "I've only just got rid of one rival in Steve Barrington. I don't want to land myself with another."

Kathryn pulled away slightly, staring up into his face. "Steve was never your rival, just an old friend I turned to because I couldn't handle my feelings for you. Of course you would have known all this a lot sooner," she admonished, "if you'd replied to my message."

His brows arched in puzzlement. "What are you talking about?"

Surprised, Kathryn described her talk with Douglas Talbot and his promise to relay a message to Gerard.

"Which I never received." Gerard frowned, a coldness creeping into his expression. "That blunder has cost us dear."

More likely a deliberate act, Kathryn mused, an image of Sarah's catlike face appearing before her. But unwilling to dwell further on unhappiness, she said "Well, we're together now . . ."

Gerard's eyes glinted down at her lovingly. "And

we don't want to waste any more time, my dearest, darling Kate . . ."

The silky words exhilarated Kathryn's senses, and she laced her fingers through his auburn hair to draw his face close, her lips moving against his as they seemed to become one, their hearts beating the same uneven rhythm.

At the sound of the phone ringing they drew apart reluctantly, Gerard hurrying to the far end of the room to snatch up the receiver before the caller hung up. She could catch little of the conversation, but when he returned to her she was alarmed to see him looking anxious.

"It's all right, Kate," he said quickly, reading her thoughts. "That wasn't about my mother, but it was an unwelcome call, all the same. I'm afraid they've hit some problems in Alaska. They really need me back there as soon as possible."

Kathryn's heart sank as he sat beside her, and she turned to him anxiously. "When will you have to go?"

"In a few days." Kathryn's face showed her distress and he took both her hands in his. "I know it's difficult, darling. I want to stay here with you more than anything in the world, but there are safety issues at stake over there and a lot of people are relying on me."

"I understand that. . . ." And she did—but it was

so hard. They'd only just come together, and now they were to be separated.

"Hey." He gripped her chin, raising her eyes to meet his. "We'll be together again soon."

A sudden thought struck her. "Would you like me to stay on here?" she asked. "I could be getting on with your mother's commission."

"Good heavens, no," he returned forcefully. "I wouldn't sleep a wink at the thought of you here alone. I'm sure the best thing is for you to return to Hollinswood, where your family is. I'll join you there as soon as possible. But I promise you this," he added, his expression sobering. "Once I've seen to my immediate obligations, I'm going to do some-thing about my crazy workaholic lifestyle. And we're going to plan a more settled life, Kate, one that will incorporate both our careers."

The warm glow in Kathryn's cheeks reached her heart as she snuggled against the folds of his shirt. She was still trying to take in the fact that Gerard loved her. Talk of their future together might be a little premature but it was reassuring that he be-lieved there was some way of melding their life-styles together to suit them both. There would have to be. She was head over heels in love with the man.

Before they left Ireland, they visited Marsha at the nursing home and found her in a private suite, a large apartment that looked as though it could have been transplanted from a posh hotel, fitted with country-style furniture and acres of deep piled carpet. Marsha was seated at the writing desk by the French windows, which opened directly onto rolling green lawns edged by beds of pansies, whose open, velvet faces were an early harbinger of spring.

She turned at their approach, her face radiant. "Darling," she cried, hands outstretched. Kathryn took one hand and bent to kiss her, relieved to see her looking so clear-eyed and well.

Greetings over, Marsha rang for refreshments and led her guests to the couch in the center of the room, taking the armchair opposite. "I'm so glad you could come to see me before you left, Kathryn," she said. "I was so disappointed when our time together was cut short."

"I would have come sooner," Kathryn replied, "but the doctors wanted to keep you all to themselves."

"Oh, them." Marsha dismissed the whole medical profession with a wave of her hand. "They make too much fuss."

"How are you feeling now," Kathryn went on. "You look absolutely marvelous."

"And I feel it—which makes me a perfect sham. Coming here has been a real tonic." She flashed a grateful smile at her son. "I was so pleased to leave that depressing hospital and I've met a great crowd.

Really," she lowered her voice confidingly, "this place is run like a country club. They have the good taste to keep all the medical facilities out of sight!"

Kathryn joined in the laughter, enjoying the banter that then took place between mother and son as Gerard insisted that Marsha would soon have the place running to her satisfaction and staff and patients alike dancing to her tune. "He has a wicked tongue," said Marsha, turning to Kathryn in a mock bid for support. Kathryn agreed smilingly, Marsha's next words catching her off guard. "I do hope he's been taking good care of you since he's been in charge of Fitzalan House?"

Cheeks scarlet, Kathryn mumbled an affirmative, managing to avoid Gerard's eyes though she sensed his deep amusement. Kathryn was spared further embarrassment by the arrival of refreshments, and the conversation turned into general chit-chat. All too soon it was time to go.

"Goodbye, my dear," said Marsha kissing Kathryn on both cheeks. "I'll be in touch as soon as I'm back home. Then we'll see about completing the commission."

Marsha closed the door behind her visitors, her mind alive with speculation. Something was going on between those two, she was sure of it. They had sat side by side, studiously avoiding eye and body contact, but they couldn't fool her! She knew what love was, and there was no disguising the look in

Gerard's eyes as he looked, oh so casually, in Kathryn's direction. A smile lit Marsha's features as she considered Kathryn as a prospective daughter-in-law. Such a bright and warm personality and so different from those glamorous cardboard cutouts Gerard had been used to squiring around. And how appropriate that she should be redheaded, Marsha mused, thinking of the Celtic coloring in the Fitzalan line. She crossed to the writing table and seated herself, an image of bouncing, bright-haired grandchildren delighting her mind's eye.

Chapter Nine

They had just announced Kathryn's flight over the airport loudspeaker which caused her to cling on to Gerard all the more. Imminent tears prickled the back of her eyelids as she admonished herself for her lack of control. You're not parting for life, she told herself repeatedly, but the sense of loss was already acute and she hadn't set foot on the plane yet. "If only I knew when you were coming to Hollinswood," she breathed, "it would be a little easier to bear."

Gerard's hands cupped her face; his fingers threaded through her tangled curls as he looked down at her. "I'll telephone you as soon as I can," he promised. "Take care, my darling and . . ." He slid a leather ring box into her left hand and closed her fingers over it. "I want you to have this. It belonged to my great-grandmother and is in my gift."

He smiled, answering the question in her widened brown eyes. "Only to be worn by Fitzalan women." His lips captured hers in a slow, tantalizing kiss as though he wanted to burn the shape of her soft lips into his memory, and then he was turning away without another word and Kathryn was hurrying to the departure gate, one clenched hand rubbing her moist eyes while the other clutched the small leather box as though it was a good luck talisman.

She did not look inside the box until she was airborne. The maroon leather lid clicked open, and she lifted out the antique ring, holding it aloft between thumb and forefinger. Her breath caught as she took in the delicate workmanship of the fine spun golden band woven into Celtic knots and studded with tiny twinkling diamonds and sapphires. It's sentimental value was far higher than any monetary worth; it was a family heirloom and Gerard had given it to her! Fully conscious of its symbolism, Kathryn returned the ring to the faded crimson silk of its case and put it in her jacket pocket, vowing not to wear it until Gerard was able to slip it on her finger himself.

The plane banked, tilting slightly as Kathryn looked through the window at the green panorama spread below like a checkered tablecloth. She didn't know when she'd return to Ireland, but she hoped it would be soon. In a short space of time the country and its people had touched her heart, and one of them had captured it completely. She could only hope her separation from Gerard would be as brief as possible.

It seemed strange at first, settling down to routine at Hollinswood Stables. So much had happened she felt as though she had been reborn, yet she did not tell anyone of the momentous events in Ireland. Her romance with Gerard was too young to be exposed to the pressure of speculation from family and friends, she told herself. Best to keep it under wraps for now.

Yet she often woke in the early hours, her longing for Gerard like an acute physical pain, her mind prey to all manner of uncertainties. What were Gerard's true feelings toward her? He had professed love, but he had not proposed—did he see their feelings for each other in the same way she did?

Then she would recall the look in his eyes as they had bid farewell at the airport. At that moment of separation she had known the strength of his feelings and, much reassured, she would settle back to sleep, angry with herself for her lapse into old fears.

Harry and Jean often asked about Marsha's illness and progress but made only passing references to Gerard. David, however, showed more curiosity and he tackled Kathryn on the subject one morning when he was helping her to groom Jasper.

"How did you and Gerard get along, Kath, when it was only the, er, two of you?"

"Fine," said Kathryn shortly, pulling a little sharply at Jasper's mane with the body brush.

"Just fine?" David queried teasingly. "Only you must have spent quite a lot of time in each other's company."

"Mmm," Kathryn mumbled, her head lowered over her task.

"Well," David persisted, "how did you pass the time?"

"By professing undying love!" Kathryn threw the body brush down and turned to glare at her cousin.

"I thought so," David chortled, making no further pretense to brush Jasper's tail as he leaned against his hindquarters, arms folded. "I always knew you two were meant for each other."

"Since when did you become an expert on romance?" Kathryn remarked, annoyed at herself for revealing so much.

"Since I noticed Gerard mooning about the stables, more interested in staring up at your window than riding Sebastian. I tried to put him off with tales of your misspent youth, but it seemed to make him keener than ever." He laughed at the indignant look on Kathryn's face. "Anyway, Kath, why the secrecy?"

"Well, for one thing, Aunt Jean is ready to send

out wedding invitations if I so much as look at a man." A frown crossed her face. "I don't want that sort of pressure, not at this early stage."

"I doubt if Gerard will need much encouragement," said David, with the cheerful confidence of one who was adept at avoiding matrimony himself. "He's been after you for a long time but you were too stubborn to see it. I can see him racing you to the altar."

Kathryn smiled at her cousin's bluntly worded vote of confidence. She wished she could share his certainty, but that would never happen until she was in Gerard's arms and he was asking her to share his future.

She had been back just over a week now and she had not heard from him. How much longer would she have to wait? She longed to hear his voice, wanted to know when she could see him again. And if he didn't contact her . . . ?

The next day she was helping Jean with a batch of baking when the phone rang. Jean answered, her voice rising as she turned to her niece. "It's for you, it's Gerard. From America!"

Flustered Kathryn sped out the door, flour rising in a dust cloud from her hands as she gestured to her aunt. "I'll take it in the hall."

"Hello," she said into the mouthpiece. Then, as

she heard the other phone click off, she changed tone. "Darling, how are you?"

"Missing you madly." His voice crackled toward her and her heart flipped over. "If I weren't working so hard I'd never sleep. But I've got good news— I'm coming to Hollinswood on Sunday!"

"Darling, that's wonderful!" Kathryn hugged herself with delight. Only five more days and they would be together! Her voice bubbled along the wires. "I can't wait! How long will you be able to stay?"

"That will rather depend on you," he said enigmatically, and Kathryn's brows rose. What could he mean? "Come up to the Manor," he went on. "I should be back by midday and I would love to find you waiting for me."

"I'll be there," she promised.

"And Kathryn," he added mischievously, "leave the rest of the day free."

She agreed, laughing, before replacing the receiver and glancing tentatively toward the closed kitchen door. She would have to fend off Aunt Jean's questions, although her private life might have to go public after this weekend. Her thoughts echoed his words—*that will depend on you.*

On Sunday morning Kathryn contemplated her wardrobe for the umpteenth time and wondered what to wear. She was meeting the man she loved after an agonizing separation, and she wanted to look her feminine best.

In the end she opted for a sleeveless turquoise dress in a delicate filmy cotton, with a figure-hugging crossover bodice and a gathered waist that flared into a full skirt. Deciding to deck herself out with fun costume jewelry, she wound a string of chunky beads marbled in gold and turquoise around her neck and added matching earrings, which flashed and glittered as she flicked her head from side to side in a sudden gesture of happiness. She slipped on a white jacket and high-heeled sandals and set off, thankful, as she walked through the stableyard, that Harry and Jean were out for the afternoon and unable to query her actions.

A few minutes later she was pressing the bell at the Manor with more self-assurance than she had been able to muster at her last visit. Her confidence almost faltered, however, when Douglas Talbot himself opened the door, dismay clearly written across his face. "Miss Beaumont," he said, in an unconvincing display of enthusiasm. "How nice."

"Mr. Fitzalan is expecting me," Kathryn told him, holding her ground. "He asked me to wait here for his arrival."

"I see." Douglas opened the door marginally wider and she slipped inside just as a phone rang shrilly in his office on their left. He dashed inside to answer it, returning almost directly, his face wreathed in a broad smile and his manner noticeably warmer. "Sorry to leave you, my dear, but that was Gerard on the car phone. He's stuck in a traffic jam—he'll be at least an hour. Come into my secretary's office," he added, noting the dismay on her face. "I'll have refreshments sent in, and the time will fly. You'll see."

Kathryn followed him through, sank into a deeply cushioned armchair, and selected a glossy magazine from the coffee table. Douglas contacted the kitchen on the house phone, then turned to his guest with a smile.

"Coffee and sandwiches will be brought directly. Make yourself at home, and if you need me, I'll be next door catching up on work."

He went through to the adjoining office and Kathryn settled down to wait, each minute passing slowly while Gerard's face rose before her. She glanced continually at her watch.

The arrival of food was a welcome diversion, and while she was eating and drinking, she heard loud footsteps stomp across the hallway and a door slam. A deeply accented voice begin to harangue Douglas, whose measured replies could hardly be heard at all.

A moment later she heard both men leave the office and cross the hallway, leaving complete silence in their wake. Unable to hear the details of the conversation, Kathryn guessed at a domestic dispute. She wondered how adept Douglas was at kitchen politics.

The insistent tones of a phone rang in the office next door. No other line was ringing—it was probably Gerard ringing through on Douglas's personal line—and Douglas was on his way to the kitchens!

She hurried into the adjoining office and had almost reached the desk at the far end of the room when her heel got caught in the carpet. She fell forward, outstretched hands sliding across the shiny surface of the desk as she knocked the phone from its connection and pushed the entire contents of the desk on to the floor.

"Oh, no!" Winded, she pulled herself upright, reconnected the phone, then set about restacking the folders which had been thrown into a heap.

One large sheet of paper folded into four had slipped from its portfolio, and as she bent to retrieve it, handwritten words on the back alerted her: "Proposed development of Hollinswood Paddocks."

With trembling fingers she opened out the paper on the desk. She had become accustomed to looking over planning applications at Parish Council meetings, and a quick glance told her all she needed to know. The Manor House would not be affected, but what was planned for the land surrounding it was a nightmare.

The grazing land, on which their business depended, was to become some sort of electronic village. Units for teleworkers were to be built and serviced by roads and parking lots, which would take what was left of their green pastures.

Kathryn's eyes lowered; the right-hand bottom corner of the plan was emblazoned with the Fitzalan logo and it was dated three weeks ago.

She felt as though she had been punched in the stomach. She clutched at the edge of the desk to steady herself, breathing deeply in an effort to steady her nerves, her heart hammering in her ears so loudly she could barely think.

One thing was painfully clear. The date on the plan proved this was no out-of-date proposal, long since abandoned. This was on stream, and Fitzalan Enterprises had been preparing the groundwork while Gerard had been telling her he loved her!

A door slammed in the far reaches of the house, pulling her out of her reverie. She replaced the plan in its portfolio and slipped it between the other folders on the desk. No one must suspect she had seen the proposal. She wanted to catch Gerard unawares, but on her home territory, not here.

She left, without seeing anyone, reaching her apartment in record time. Throwing her jacket and shoes off, she stood by her long living room window looking down at the deserted stableyard. David had taken a party out hacking, and the girls were teaching a group of schoolchildren in the paddocks.

She felt very alone as she contemplated the consequences of the plan she had just seen.

No wonder the company had fobbed them off with an annual lease. When their current arrangement expired in a few months time, they could be kicked off without any compensation, leaving the way open for development.

Her distress deepened as she thought of how Gerard had stolen her heart and charmed her family while plotting behind their backs to destroy their home and business. Well, he hadn't won yet. She would squeeze every emotion she had ever felt for him out of her mind, and would fight his company tooth and nail to make sure their proposal never went through!

She knew he would follow her. Less than an hour after she returned home, there was an impatient knock at the door. She opened it to find Gerard staring down at her, a hint of anxiety shadowing his gray eyes. "Darling, there you are. Douglas said you just left without a word. Are you all right? Is there anything wrong?"

"There's a lot wrong." She contemplated him in silence, his tall figure clad in a charcoal gray suit, a frown now darkening his brow. She wondered that she could look at him with such hatred in her heart.

His right hand moved toward her. "Don't touch me!" The words flashed out as she edged away from him, her hands knotted tightly by her side. "Keep away from me."

"Am I allowed to know why?" He stepped over the threshold, slamming the door behind him in a fierce gesture.

"I know what you intend to do with Hollinswood Paddocks," she said, her voice hoarse from the effort of forcing words from a dry mouth. "I came across the plans this morning at the Manor."

"Enlighten me." His shoulders rose in a derisive shrug. "What do I intend to do with them?"

His pretended ignorance infuriated her. "You intend to build on them." The words spluttered from her in a quick, accusatory list. "Units for teleworkers, new roads, new parking lots, until the whole lot is under concrete and my family is ruined!"

He flinched under her onslaught and she knew a moment of pure delight. Good—that had shaken him. He'd had no idea she'd rumbled him.

He thrust his right hand wearily through his spiky locks. "Darling, there must be some mistake. There's no intention of developing your grazing land, and there never has been."

"Don't darling me!" Keen disappointment swept over her as she realized he was still trying to plead ignorance. "And don't patronize me," she said thinly. "I can read a planning brief. I know what I saw."

"Then show me." He moved closer, his dark brows drawn together, his mouth in a tight, straight line. "Come back with me now," he coaxed. "We'll look at what you saw together, and sort this out once and for all."

She almost wavered, undermined by the intensity of the gaze fixed upon her and by his nearness, which was already exercising its familiar, potent magic.

She dragged her eyes away from his face, her fingernails digging into her palms hard enough to draw blood. "No! I won't be lied to anymore." She drew herself up, backbone rigid, and never knew where she found the strength to speak the next words. "You're the head of the company, Gerard, you must know what's planned for Hollinswood. You've tricked me and my family, and I can't forgive you." Her voice broke then gathered strength, "I don't want to see you again . . . ever."

She turned from him but he was not to be dismissed so easily. One hand gripped her shoulder, pulling her around to face him. "I don't know what all this is about, but you've blown it, Kathryn. I came here today to ask you to marry me—like some poor sap, I thought you loved me. Obviously not. You've got some crazy notion in your head and I'm condemned without a hearing. Well, if that's how you want it—you've got it."

He released her suddenly, and she began to shake uncontrollably as he swept out of the room. She could hardly take in the enormity of what had happened to her, and her first thought after he left was that she had forgotten to return the ring which she had received with such hope in her heart only a short while ago. Her fingers closed over the ring which hung on a fine gold chain around her neck and, in an angry gesture, she tore it from her, no longer willing to wear a tangible reminder of her lost love. Tomorrow she would send it back to him, she decided, and the last link between them would be at an end.

In spite of her grief she knew she could not afford to give in to her emotions; she would need a clear head to fight the proposed development. Her aunt and uncle must not know of the threat to their livelihood—it would play havoc with Uncle Harry's health—but she would need help, and David was her obvious ally.

She told him what had occurred later that evening, warning him to keep the knowledge to himself for the time being.

"Poor Kath." He gave her hand a brief squeeze. "You've had a terrible time."

"We're all going to have a tough time if this development goes through. It'd ruin the stables."

David grimaced. "Just how likely is it to succeed?" he asked. "We're in the middle of a National Park, with strict building controls. Surely it wouldn't get planning permission?"

"I'm not so sure," Kathryn admitted. "The company could point out that it would provide a lot of new jobs."

"Which the area desperately needs," David added.

"Precisely. And if the company scales down the proposal and throws in some perfectly legal inducements . . ."

"It might just slip through the planning net," David completed, his brow furrowed. "It's a chance we can't take, Kath, but what can we do before they show their hand? There's no planning application in at the moment or else we'd know about it."

"Do some digging," Kathryn suggested, "and see if we can find out when the company intends to move on this."

"I've got a contact up at the Manor," David said thoughtfully. "I could ask her to check this out for us."

"Is this the mysterious girlfriend you keep under wraps?"

"Just a friend," David said loftily. "In the meantime, Kath, it might be useful if you could visit the planning offices and see what you can find out."

But as it happened, Kathryn never made it to the planning offices. While in an art supplies shop in

Buxton one quiet Wednesday afternoon, she was surprised when a small car drew to a halt outside and Douglas Talbot got out, glanced around the street, and then crossed the road to enter the hotel opposite. Douglas rarely went anywhere without a chauffeur-driven company limousine, and his behavior was distinctly furtive.

Making her mind up swiftly Kathryn followed in his footsteps, slipped into the hotel foyer and began to browse through the tourist brochures on view while edging slowly toward the door to the bar.

A full-length mirror with a heavy gilt frame was strategically placed opposite the open doorway of the bar, and the angle of its view gave Kathryn a chance to gaze unseen at Douglas Talbot and his guest.

He was deep in conversation with the chief planning officer. She had no way of knowing what they were saying, but she was struck once more by Douglas's secretive air.

For the first time doubts as to Gerard's guilt began to bubble to the surface. Was it possible that Talbot was playing a lone game, planning to deceive his own boss as well as her family? Or was she simply clutching at straws? She left before she could be discovered, anxious to discuss her new theory with her cousin.

David must have been doing thorough research for he was out all evening and it wasn't until coffee time the following morning that she found him alone.

Excitedly she told him of what she had seen in Buxton, expressing her new doubts as to Talbot's integrity.

"I've been getting the same sort of feedback from the Manor. According to my contact no one there knows of any plan to build on our land. In fact, my friend is pretty certain that Gerard would disapprove strongly if he knew of it."

If he knew of it. Kathryn winced as she recalled how she had refused his offer to investigate. Resolutely she drew her mind back to the matter in hand. "That would account for Talbot's secrecy. No doubt he wants to present Gerard with a *fait accompli*. Once planning permission has been granted and builders contracted, the company can't pull out without losing a lot of money." Shakily she raised one hand to her brow. "David, this is all supposition. We've no real evidence to go on."

"I know, and we must do something about it." David brought his clenched fist down on the table with a thud. "The guy's trying to ruin our livelihood."

"Ask your friend for help," Kathryn urged. "She's on the inside. If she could obtain some evidence, anything at all, we can go to Gerard."

"I'll try, Kath. I'm seeing her tonight. I'll do my best for us."

There was nothing more to be said. Kathryn tried to forget their troubles as she went about her daily tasks, but it was difficult and her thoughts kept returning to the memory of Gerard's face, hardened with shock as she'd launched into him with her accusations. If their suspicions were correct and they could prove Gerard's innocence, would he ever forgive her lack of trust?

That night she went to bed early and fell into an uncomfortable, heavy slumber. The next thing she knew a light was shining in her eyes and a familiar voice was ordering her to wake up.

She struggled to a sitting position, rubbed her sleep-swollen eyes, then realized her cousin was perched at the bottom of her bed. "What are you playing at," she hissed. "What time is it?"

"Two-thirty in the morning and you need to get up sharpish." He crossed to the door, throwing the words over his shoulder as he went. "We need to go up to Hollinswood Manor, Kath. Right now!"

Kathryn hurried to keep up with David's long strides as she attempted to take in his rather rushed explanation.

"My friend is certain Talbot is attempting to commit fraud and that we'll find the evidence inside his office. Unfortunately, when I arrived at the Manor earlier this evening I found her packing—she's just been recalled to the States."

David turned to his cousin with a flash of his blue eyes. "She needs us to follow through for her, Kath. She daren't trust any other employee at the moment, and doesn't want Talbot to know he's under suspicion. That's why we're going in for all this cloak-and-dagger stuff. She's told me exactly what I need to do. Are you willing to help?"

"Of course. I'd never let you do this on your own."

"Good, because I need your help to get into the Manor. Apparently the house is alarmed except for the kitchen porch, which has been excluded because it's awaiting demolition—you can still open the side window from the outside. I'd never get through that small gap, but you would. Then you can let me in through the porch door. Are you quite happy with that?"

"I certainly am. We'll do what we have to do to expose Talbot." And exonerate Gerard, she added to herself, wondering what tonight's escapade would mean for herself and the man she loved.

Chapter Ten

For the second time in her adult life Kathryn made an illicit entry into Hollinswood Manor through the small porch window, and this time no strong hands greeted her, only the cold kiss of the quarry tiles as she tumbled to the floor. She was up immediately, pulling back the door bolts and drawing her cousin inside.

"Good girl. Now let's go, we've no time to lose." He led the way through the kitchen, the narrow beam of their flashlight picking out obstacles in their path until they came to the door in the passageway where they paused for a while, bodies poised for flight, as they took in the sounds of the sleeping household. Nothing stirred except for old timbers which creaked and settled in an age-old ritual.

It was safe to continue. They padded down darkened corridors, their sneakers making little impact on the thick carpeting, until they reached the sanctuary of Douglas's office.

Kathryn closed the door, leaning against it with relief. She felt more secure in this enclosed space, the heavy damask curtains closed to the night air, the solid door between herself and the rest of the household. She joined David over at the desk.

"We can risk a light, it won't show," he said, switching on the green shaded desk lamp. He stood back, his glance encompassing Douglas's desk. "Apparently, this is where Talbot keeps all his personal papers—the drawers are locked at all times and not even his secretary has access. However, my friend seemed quite confident she would be able to obtain the key for us." He flashed a smile at his cousin. "I didn't inquire as to what methods she would use, but if she succeeded, the key should be somewhere in this in-tray." There was an untidy jumble of papers in a wire basket on the right hand corner of the desk and as he spoke David began to look through them. Next moment, with a low whoop of joy he was holding a small brass key aloft.

He unlocked the top right hand drawer first and as he pulled it open they peered down, heads close together. Kathryn was the first to voice her disappointment. "There's nothing there, nothing but pencils and pens."

"Let's try the other drawers." Yet they too proved empty of anything of interest, and after they'd finished their feverish search, David straightened, one hand brushing through his blond mop as he voiced his frustration. "There's nothing here, Kath. Has Talbot covered his tracks because he knows we're on to him? Or have we got everything quite wrong?"

Kathryn couldn't bear to relinquish the hope that had been growing within her, that Gerard might not be implicated in the betrayal of her family. She shook her head as though to dispel any notion that they were on the wrong track. "I feel sure Talbot is guilty," she affirmed. "We've got to think our way through this, David."

She stepped back, frowning, as she glanced over the elegant antique desk. "Something's wrong," she murmured.

David exhaled sharply. "It sure is, but we can't hang around here forever discussing it. We—"

"No," she cut in, "I mean something's wrong with the proportions of this desk. Look." She gestured toward the right-hand drawer. "That drawer is much narrower than the one on the left."

"So?"

"Well, this desk looks Georgian, and everything they made at that time was symmetrical. Both drawers should look exactly alike, unless . . ."

"Yes?" David prompted. "What are you getting at?"

"I think there might be a secret drawer," said Kathryn excitedly. "Remember the one Uncle John had in a desk similar to this? He used to show it to us when we were kids, and we used to snigger behind his back and say it was full of old love letters."

Realization dawned on her cousin's face. "I think you might be on to something, Kath."

He pulled the right-hand drawer out and bent low over it. "Now, if I can just remember how to release the catch." He reached inside with his gloved hand, frowning in concentration as his fingers sought out any sign that there was another compartment above the drawer space. Next moment his expression turned to one of jubilation as there was a click and a slim drawer glided out. There was a brown manila folder inside and excitedly they spread its contents over the desk. Unfolding a large sheet of paper, Kathryn recognized the plan she had already seen. "That's what I saw when I was here before," she said.

David cursed under his breath, "There won't be a blade of grass left if that goes through. Let's see what else we've got."

The development brief was supplemented by detailed costings and profit forecasts. "It'd take an accountant to sort this lot out," David grumbled but Kathryn peered closer, her brow creased.

"There is something fishy going on, David—look." She pointed to the documents. "None of the profits are being attributed to Fitzàlan Enterprises. Other corporations are named—companies I've never heard of."

David gave a low whistle as the implications of what she'd said sank in. "You're right, Kath. It looks as though Talbot's private enterprise is intended for his own pocket." He slammed his fist down on the desk. "We've got enough, Kath. We can copy these documents and take the evidence to Gerard."

"There's a photocopier next door in the secretary's office," Kathryn told him. "So let's get a move on and then get out of here." They went through and, after completing their task, replaced the original documents in the folder and returned it to its hiding place.

"No one should know we've been investigating," David remarked, as he locked each drawer and then threw the key back into the in-tray. "Talbot may think it strange to find his key here, but, hopefully, he'll assume he left it here in a fit of absentmindedness."

"Now all we've got to do is get out without being discovered," Kathryn said grimly. "Let's go!"

This time Kathryn crossed the hallway with shoulders squared and head high. Gerard was innocent! Her heart sang with the knowledge while her mind wrestled with the problem of how to win him back.

When he sees our evidence he'll realize how black it looked from my point of view, she reasoned. Surely he would forgive her lapse in trust if she could convince him that she truly loved him. And she would convince him, she determined, her hands involuntarily clenching at her side—the days of doubt and mistrust were well and truly over.

They reached the kitchen porch and Kathryn let David out, locked the door, then slipped out through the window, sliding it shut behind her. The grounds were eerily silent, and to avoid rustling the loose chippings of the driveway, they walked along the grass verge, guided only by watery light of a half moon.

They didn't speak until they were well past the gates. Then Kathryn broke the silence with, "Now how do we go about contacting Gerard without Talbot knowing?"

"Through my friend. I have a contact number in New York and instructions on when to phone. Then the ball's in their court. I expect Gerard will come over himself to sort things out."

"I hope so," Kathryn said. I hope so, she repeated to herself silently.

When she reached home Kathryn collapsed, fully clothed, onto the bed, exhausted by nervous tension, to be woken only a few hours later by the sounds of stableyard bustle. Bleary-eyed she settled herself in her studio to await news.

David arrived breathlessly in midafternoon to say that he'd only just managed to get through to New York. "Gerard's coming over. We're to sit tight, keep quiet, and await word from the Manor."

"When's he coming?" Kathryn asked, her face revealing a mixture of delight and apprehension.

"It's going to take him a while to get away, but he should be here by the weekend."

Another five days! How was she going to bear it? "You've got some humble pie to eat," her cousin went on blithely, "when you two meet up again."

Kathryn's mouth twisted into a wry smile. "Thanks for reminding me!"

"I'm sure he'll forgive you," David went on, in a clumsy attempt at consolation. "After all, it looks as though you've helped to uncover some pretty crooked dealings."

What do balance sheets have to do with hurt feelings and damaged pride? Kathryn wondered miserably. What if Gerard found it impossible to forgive her? She found the prospect of life without him unbearable to contemplate and turned away from her cousin, blinking back sudden, hot tears.

The days crawled toward the weekend and, much to her fury, Kathryn found she would have to spend Saturday in York, visiting a prospective venue for an exhibition.

The day went well, too well, for the gallery owner insisted on taking her out to dine. Kathryn engineered an early meal, made her excuses as soon as possible, and by nine thirty was on the road back to Hollinswood.

It was almost midnight by the time she reached the stables, but on impulse, she drove past, following the road uphill toward the Manor.

She stopped at the top of the hill and climbed out, leaning against her car as she looked through the gap in the hedge that gave her a clear view of the upper stories of the house. Her pulse jerked; a lamp shone in the third room of the east wing. Gerard was back.

She knew what she had to do, but if she pondered too long she'd lose her nerve. She set off again, driving in through the Manor gates and drawing to a halt outside the front door. After getting out she rang the bell impatiently, her palms moistening at the thought that soon, very soon she would see Gerard again.

The door swung open to reveal Sarah in an evening dress in a soft, silky material in cornflower blue.

"Kathryn!" Her finely penciled brows rose over her rounded blue eyes. "This is rather a late visit."

"I . . . I'm sorry to disturb you," Kathryn stammered. "I just wondered if Gerard was—"

"Gerard's had a very long day. I'm sure you'll be able to see him tomorrow."

Kathryn's eyes fell suddenly onto the large diamond ring on Sarah's left hand. Sarah's eyes followed her glance.

"I see you've rumbled us, Kathryn. It was going to be a surprise but now you're here, come and join the celebration."

She reached forward but Kathryn shrank from her. "No, I have to go now . . . I'm sorry . . ." She turned and ran, too stunned to cry, too frozen to feel anything at all.

She knew she could not stay in Hollinswood any longer. She could not meet Gerard the next day without revealing her breaking heart, and on the short journey back to the stables, she made a snap decision to go to London, knowing that Molly, her roommate from art college days, would put her up.

Back at the stables she packed a small suitcase then slipped a note to David through the letterbox of the main house on her way to the car. She didn't mention where she was going, just that she would phone when she was settled.

Tension kept her mind crystal clear on the long drive down the highway but with only light traffic to deal with she had too much time to brood. She couldn't blame Gerard for turning to Sarah after she'd rejected him so cruelly, but pain shredded her heart every time she recalled the expression on Sarah's face when she had looked at her engagement ring.

When Kathryn arrived on her friend's doorstep, ashen-faced in the early hours, Molly asked few questions then left her to sleep the day away.

Kathryn spent the next few days mooching around the flat while Molly was out, unwilling to contact her family or even to think of what was happening in Hollinswood. She evaded her friend's questions, and when Molly suggested putting off her plans to go away from the weekend so that she would not be alone, Kathryn dissuaded her, convinced that solitude was just what she needed right now.

However, the weekend loomed emptily before her and Saturday night found Kathryn watching a film on television that she had no interest in whatsoever.

The doorbell rang. She hurried to the door and unlocked it, only to find it pushed wide open as David strode into the hallway. "You've led us a merry dance, Kath!"

He went into the living room and threw himself on to the small sofa. Kathryn followed, feeling like a child who'd been caught out in a misdemeanor. "I suppose Molly told you where I was," she said defensively.

"Too right. She was concerned about you, as we all were."

"Well, there's no need." Kathryn seated herself opposite. "As I said in my letter, I just want time to myself—to think."

"What about? It was a weird time to do a vanishing trick, when so many things were happening."

"What has happened about the land?"

"A lot," he returned shortly, "and everything's going to be fine—but I don't want to go into details right now. I want to know what's wrong with you, because something is very wrong."

She knew David's stubbornness—after all she shared the same family trait—and knew she had better tell him everything. She drew a long breath and relayed what had happened, her voice trailing away into silence as she sat back, totally unprepared for his reaction.

"Kathryn, I could shake you, sometimes. It's me that's engaged to Sarah—not Gerard!"

Kathryn's jaw dropped. Of course, it all made perfect sense once she thought about it. "So, Sarah is the mysterious girlfriend," her voice rose higher, "and the inside contact who did so much to help us?"

When David nodded in affirmation, Kathryn said, "Then why didn't you say so? Why so much secrecy?"

"Sarah's price for helping us was absolute discretion. I couldn't tell anyone of her involvement, not even you. As for the personal side . . ." He shrugged, grinning sheepishly. "We've been seeing each other since New Year's Eve. I didn't tell you because you didn't seem very keen on her and, what's more, you'd have bent my ears with sisterly advice."

"Oh, David," Kathryn sighed, "if only you'd been more open."

"Sorry," he said contritely, "but how was I to know you'd jump to the wrong conclusion?"

"It was hardly surprising when she was standing there with a huge diamond on her finger. When did you decide to become engaged, anyway?"

"That very night. I proposed on impulse. The ring, by the way, was Granny Robertson's. I thought you might have recognized it."

"I was too shocked to look at it properly." It was a lot to take in, but the least she could do was congratulate her cousin. She leaned forward and clasped his hands. "Sarah and I got off to a bad start, but once I get to know her properly, I'm sure I'll like her. I hope you will both be very happy— really I do."

They, at least, had a chance of happiness while she, having doubted Gerard for a second time, had none. Her vision blurred and she went into the kitchen for a tissue, returning just in time to see David heading for the door.

"Just going out for a while, Kath. See you later."

"But why—" The door slammed shut on her words. What was he up to? She shrugged, returning to the kitchen to make coffee.

She began to grind the beans, then forgot her task, staring out through the kitchen window at the uninspiring view of slate roofs, her mind meandering, going over the news David had brought . . .

"Make one for me while you're at it!"

Kathryn whipped around, the small grinder clattering to the floor, to find Gerard leaning against the door jamb, arms folded. The floor seemed to tilt beneath her feet as she took in the fact that the man she loved was only a few feet away.

"Well, Kathryn?" A slow smile lit his features, his eyes sparking an unmistakable message.

Her mind blanked. "How did you get in?" she asked nervously, palms moistening as she backed against the sink.

His smile widened to show his white, even teeth. "David left the door open."

"I see. A conspiracy."

"Right down the line. We came here together. We thought you'd be more likely to open up to David and we'd find out what was troubling you."

"So." Kathryn squared her shoulders, a characteristic twinkle beginning to reassert itself in her eyes. "I was set up?"

"Sure were, lady."

Kathryn never knew who moved first, but the next moment she was wrapped in Gerard's arms and he was burying his face in her hair, murmuring her name over and over. She lifted her face to his, coiling her arms around his neck as he swung her into his arms, strode with her into the sitting room, and lowered himself onto the sofa where he settled her on his lap.

It was no time for words. His mesmeric silver eyes spoke only of longing, and her skin prickled. His lips swooped to savor the fullness of her mouth.

They were lost in a world of their own. Then his lips broke from hers. "Don't ever leave me again," he murmured, his ragged breath warm against her cheek.

His words reminded her painfully of their bitter separation, and she disentangled herself to sit upright. Her hand splayed on his chest as she looked up at him. "Gerard, we must talk."

He grimaced wryly but held his hands up in a gesture of resignation as she continued. "I accused you of terrible things last time we met. Can you forgive me?"

"I have to admit I hated you at first," he told her bluntly. "But you know, Kate, hate is akin to love. Anyway, I returned to New York in a high old state, but when I calmed down I realized that you must have stumbled across something that needed investigating. I set up a discreet inquiry but you and David, with Sarah's help, beat me to it. When I saw what you'd uncovered I realized the extent of the man's treachery." Gerard's features hardened as he contemplated his old friend's betrayal.

Kathryn's heart stirred with sympathy. "I'm so sorry, Gerard." She ran her forefinger lightly down Gerard's cheek, outlining his tightened jaw. "I know you thought a lot of Douglas."

"Too much." He spat the words out, then captured her hand in his, pressing his lips to her fingers as he continued, his tone softening. "The trouble was, I treated him like a surrogate father when Dad died, and he took advantage of that. I gave him total control over Hollinswood, and he was all set to exploit the land and cream off some of the profits into dummy corporations he'd set up. Quite an elaborate scam."

"But he has been stopped, hasn't he?" Kathryn asked anxiously. "David didn't go into details."

"Everything's fine." He kissed her briefly on the nose. "Thanks to you and your cousin, the fraud was uncovered at an early stage. The police are involved, and the accountants are picking up the pieces of Talbot's crooked dealings."

"What's happened to him?" Kathryn asked soberly. "Is he in custody?"

"He's vanished, and with his gift for deception, I doubt if the police will ever find him. To be frank it's probably the best thing. Even after all he's done I think I'd find it quite difficult to see him go to jail. And at the end of the day"—his shoulders rose—"very little harm was done."

"Except to us," Kathryn said, "I should have trusted you, Gerard, should have accepted your word above everything. I don't know how you've been able to forgive me."

"When David showed me what you'd uncovered I realized the evidence against me had looked damning. And because I love you so much, I was all too ready to forgive you!"

He pulled her fiercely against him and for one long moment they held each other close, Kathryn murmuring his name softly as though trying to assuage the hurt she had done to this proud, strong man.

Eventually she stirred, keen to clear the air further, anxious there should be nothing left unsaid between them. "It must have been Douglas who blocked my message to you after New Year's Eve," she pointed out.

"Undoubtedly." Gerard's brows knitted. "Nothing easier than saying he'd passed the message on when he'd done no such thing. It would suit his purpose to break us up. If I was visiting Hollinswood to see you, I'd soon find out what was going on."

"And I thought it was Sarah who was trying to keep us apart," Kathryn confessed. There was one more subject she had to broach. She looked shyly into his eyes. "Do you think I was very foolish to think you and Sarah were involved?"

"Foolish to think I'd turn to her after you, yes, but when David told me, my first reaction was . . . relief." Kathryn's brows rose as he explained. "I reckoned if you were mad with jealousy, you must still have some feelings for me."

"Gerard, I've never stopped caring for you!" She forced the next few words out, her throat feeling painfully tight. "I've never stopped loving you."

His eyes sparkled like champagne. "I've waited a long time to hear those words. I've loved you madly since the first moment I saw you." He reached inside his pocket and produced a small square box that Kathryn knew well. "I've kept this close, Kate, in the hope that one day I'd be able to return it to you." He slipped it on to her finger and as Kathryn looked down at the delicate antique ring she found herself lost for words, intoxicated by a variety of emotions. Gerard stroked her soft, russet curls back from her forehead and added mischievously, "I hope our children inherit your glorious coloring, Kate."

His words had the desired effect of drawing her eyes to his. "Aren't you jumping the gun a little," she said shakily.

"Perhaps." He smiled down into her face. "How would you like to live at Hollinswood Manor?"

"I'd love to live at the Manor with you," Kathryn breathed.

"Good. I need to head the European operations now, and the Manor seems the perfect home for both of us."

Kathryn murmured her agreement, snuggling against him. "And Uncle Harry will get his lease," she went on, "and I'll be close at hand to help out when he's not well."

"Harry won't be getting any lease" Gerard said, enjoying the effect of his broadside as Kathryn's head shot up. "He'll be getting the land, lock, stock, and barrel. It will be our present to Harry and Jean on the day we get married."

Kathryn's heart filled with love as she took in the extent of his generosity. She tilted her head to one side as she shot Gerard a mischievous smile. "Is this an attempt at bribery, Mr. Fitzalan, or a marriage proposal?"

"Both. Will you be my Lady of the Manor? In short, will you be my wife, Kate?"

"Oh, yes!" She twined her slender arms around his neck and drew him close, sighing with contentment as she contemplated their present, and future, happiness.